A HOLLY FOR X-MAS

OLIVIA T. TURNER

Copyright© 2021 by Olivia T. Turner.
All rights reserved. No part of this book may be reproduced or transmitted in any form or by any means, electronic or mechanical, including emailing, photocopying, printing, recording, or by any information storage and retrieval system, without permission in writing from the author. For permission requests, email Olivia@oliviatturner.com

Please respect the author's hard work and purchase a copy. Thanks!

This is a work of fiction. Any resemblance to actual events, businesses, companies, locales or persons, living or dead, is entirely coincidental.
Contains explicit love scenes and adult language.
18+

www.OliviaTTurner.com

Edited by Karen Collins Editing
Cover Design by Olivia T. Turner

*To all my readers during this Holiday Season.
I hope you get everything you want.
Love, happiness, wine, and of course, lots of presents.*

CHAPTER ONE

Holly

"So, I'll see you tomorrow?" I ask with a smile as I wrap my big wooly scarf around my neck.

"You know what, Holly?" Mike says as he tosses a dirty pot into the huge sink. "Jeff and Karl are bringing their extended families in tomorrow to help out, so we'll be more than enough."

I feel my stomach drop.

"Why don't you stay home with your family?"

My eyes drop to the tiled floor as my cheeks heat up.

"Oh," I say as I force my eyes to look at him. I wrench out a smile. "Okay! Yeah. Great. I'll do that. You guys don't need me."

He must see the quiver in my chin or the brokenness in my eyes because he backtracks hard. "Unless you don't have any… place to go?"

I swallow hard as I struggle to force out a smile. "I have a family."

He looks at me skeptically, waiting with a look of pity in his eyes.

My fist presses against my thigh as we stare at each other awkwardly.

I could come clean. I could tell him that my father died unexpectedly three years ago, that I never knew my mother, and that my asshole brother Matthew is somewhere in Asia—Singapore I think. He doesn't answer my emails and he's never given me his phone number. I could tell him, pathetic though it is, that this soup kitchen is the closest thing to family I have. And if I'm not volunteering here on Christmas day, then I'll be all alone, watching Christmas movies in tears, which it looks like I'll now be doing.

I could say all that. But I don't.

"Okay, bye!" I quickly say before spinning on my heels and rushing out before the tears do.

"Holly, wait!" Mike calls out when I'm at the door.

"Yes?" I turn around, hope blooming inside me.

"Merry Christmas."

"Oh," I say, feeling my shoulders drop. "Thanks."

I turn and press the big heavy doors open with two hands. Cold air blasts me in the face.

It's freezing out and the snow is coming down hard. I fix my hat and trudge through the snow in the parking lot with my head hanging low. This hurts.

The holidays used to be so fun. Decorating the gingerbread house that my dad baked, but could never stick together properly. Chris sneaking Smarties that was supposed to be the lights on the roof. All three of us giving up and eating the broken pieces for dinner while laughing our butts off to Elf. Now? Now it's all different.

The holidays aren't a time of love. My heart aches throughout them. I'm lucky if I don't spend the whole day crying.

My feet are already soaked when I get to my old beater car with the foot of snow on it. I grunt as I struggle to pull open the frozen door. I finally get it open and climb in. The frozen seats are rock hard.

Starting this old piece of junk is its own adventure, but I eventually get the sad engine groaning. I'll be lucky if the heat comes on by the time I get home.

I grab the scraper off the passenger seat and get to work on the snow as my car unsuccessfully tries to heat up. A Christmas song plays on the radio and I try not to cry. I'd rather not have frozen eyelids while scraping the ice off my windshield.

Bing Crosby is singing about how great it is to be surrounded by family throughout the holidays. Geez, Bing. Stab me in the heart why don't you?

This is so depressing. I thought I could start a new tradition of volunteering on Christmas day after the drunken lonely fiasco that was last Christmas, but even they don't want me.

Maybe I'll just stay in bed and hide under the sheets, pretending that it's a normal Tuesday.

Being out here in the frigid cold, a day in a warm bed doesn't sound too bad right about now.

I get my car as clean as I can and then head back in covered in snow.

Mariah is belting out high notes about how great Christmas is and I just can't. I change it to the rock station. They proudly refuse to play any Christmas songs and that's just what I need right now. The guitar is loud and grating in my ears, but at least they're not making me feel like the most pathetic person on the planet.

My car reluctantly gets going and I pull out of the parking lot onto the road.

Wow, there's a lot of snow. It's really coming down.

I perk up in my seat and put both my hands on the wheel, ten and two. I didn't think the roads were this bad. My winter tires should have been changed a few years ago, but they're always tumbling down the list of things I need to pay for. I'm kind of regretting that decision now as I swerve a little bit on the snow-filled icy road.

The road is dark with thick forest on each side, no lights for miles.

I turn the radio off, needing my full concentration as I try to stay on the road. The plows haven't passed, but I guess they're short-staffed since it's Christmas Eve.

My heart is pounding as my car makes little jerks to each side, losing control for split seconds at a time. I hate this…

I'm far away from the soup kitchen when big headlights begin to approach in the opposite direction. I swallow hard as I white-knuckle the steering wheel.

God, they're so bright. They're blinding…

That looks like a big SUV coming.

My pulse races as the headlights get closer. Adrenaline peaks.

With the mounds of snow on each side of the road, the area to drive in has shrunken to dangerous levels. There's not a lot of room to pass each other. It's going to be close.

I suck in a breath and hold it in as my car slips to the left. "No!"

It picks the worst time to lose control. I scream as my

front bumper suddenly swerves and goes careening into the bright headlights.

The ice spins the car until my headlights are pointed on the trees and the approaching headlights are lighting me up through the passenger side window.

I scream in terror as they come closer… closer… about to smash into me.

I'll be spending Christmas in a hospital. Or in a morgue. I'll find out soon enough.

They make an abrupt turn, plunging me back into darkness as the SUV rips to its left and flies off the road into the heavy snow with a horrible sound. My car flies forward through the snowbank with a *crunch* and skids to a stop right before the trees.

I stare at the large trunk of an oak tree in front of me as I try to catch my breath. My heart is hammering in my chest. I nearly died. I could have died. What the fuck?!

When I'm able to compose myself enough to turn my head around, I see the SUV across the road stuck in the snow, headlights pointing into the other side of the forest.

I swallow hard as I grab my hat, shove it on, and rush out to check on them. Shit. They're going to be so pissed.

It's eight o'clock on Christmas Eve. They're probably headed to a family party or a night with friends and here I come with my shit car and meek existence to run them off the road and ruin it all.

I feel terrible.

My feet sink into the heavy snow as more thick flakes come down, collecting on my hat and shoulders. "Come on," I mutter as I sink to my upper thighs with every step. I'm soaked.

The road is easier to walk on, but it's even more slippery. No wonder my car went careening off it. It's pure ice under a layer of snow.

The big black SUV is parked at a weird angle. The door opens as I rush to it.

"Are you okay?" I shout as I jump into the snowbank and continue trudging forward. "I'm *so* sorry!"

A man in a suit and long jacket steps out and turns to me.

I jerk my head back in surprise when I see him. He stares at me with a heated look, falling snow slowly gathering on his black jacket and in his dark hair.

He's beautiful. Just the kind of guy I would run off the road—rich, successful, hot, and on his way to a party. One second with me in his life and that's all gone out the window. His plans are shot. So is his truck.

"I don't know what happened," I say with my voice racing. "I was trying to drive straight and I must have hit a patch of ice and then my car was turning and your lights were coming and I was so scared and there was nothing I could do…"

The words finally stop when the tears start pouring out. All of the nerves and emotions I was dealing with before mix together and I start balling in front of this handsome stranger.

Geez. Can I get any more pathetic? Seriously…

I cover my wet eyes with my gloves as my shoulders shake.

The crunching sound of his footsteps hit my ears and then I feel warm comforting arms around me, holding me close as I cry.

He's a stranger. He's probably some creep. I should push him away and run back to my car. He has no business hugging me. We don't know each other at all. It's inappropriate.

But I sink into that hug and cry into his chest. It feels so good to be held like this. It feels so good to have someone care. Even if he is a total perv.

"There's no crying on Christmas Eve," he says in a deep smooth voice that has the cold leaving my bones, replacing it with an unexpected warmth.

"There is where I come from," I say as I pull away from his chest. Crap. I got tears all over his nice tie.

He touches the bottom of my chin with his leather glove and tilts my head up until I'm looking into his eyes.

I gulp as they fixate on me.

The intensity in them is surprising. It's unexpected as he stares down at me, looking at me like no one ever has before. I don't know what to think.

The warm scent of his cologne fills my lungs and gets me all flushed. Who is this guy?

Whoever he is, he's got a lucky girl in the passenger seat of his truck. She's got to be a total knockout and one hell of a catch to be with a man like him.

He's beautiful, but not in the classic sense. If you're one of those freaks like me who get turned on by the villains in movies, then you'd understand. His face is all hard sharp edges. Narrow lines. Dark eyebrows. Heated possessive eyes that instantly tell you you're out of your league with this man.

All I can do is take heavy shaky breaths as I look up at him through my snow-dusted eyelashes.

"Are you hurt?" he asks as he grips my arms with his hands and looks me up and down.

Heat blooms within me as his eyes drag up and down my body.

Am I really getting turned on? Come on, Holly. You just ran this poor guy off the road. We're in the middle of a snowstorm and your car is fucked. Now is not the time to get these kinds of thoughts.

No matter how hard I try to shame myself, the feeling doesn't go away. It intensifies.

I've always been drawn to older men—Teachers, my dad's friend, the guy who mows his lawn shirtless down the street—those are the kind of men who have always gotten my attention, but I've never gotten theirs.

This man is different. He's looking at me in a new way. A way that's getting my toes curling in these soaked running shoes.

He must be in his early forties. I just turned twenty-two. That's a hell of an age gap, but as we stand here staring at each other… it doesn't seem to matter one bit.

"I'm okay," I say in a soft voice, not quite believing it.

Physically, I'm fine, but with him now in my life… I don't know. I might never be okay again.

CHAPTER TWO

Nate

"WHAT'S YOUR NAME?" I ask the Christmas miracle in my hands. I'm gripping her arms like I'm never going to let her go, and right now, I don't know if I'll ever be able to.

I want her.

She's already consuming me. My truck is probably stuck in the snow, but I don't even give that a passing thought. I'm fixated on her.

I'm being pulled in hard. She's so alluring. So seductively innocent. I need this girl in my life. I need this girl to *be* my life.

She's looking up at me with those rosy cheeks and those big blue Bambi eyes. *Fuck...* it's hitting a part of me that's never been hit before. A protective possessive part that is raging to life as we stand here in the snow.

It wants me to pick her up and bring her to my truck. Put her in and drive. Peel that big coat off her body and see what wonders she's hiding underneath. It wants me to take that beautiful innocence radiating off her. It wants to be *consumed* by her. And it wants it now.

"My name is Holly," she says in a voice so sweet and pure that it gets my heart aching. I've never experienced anything like this before. I'm in pain as I watch her. I'm tender all over. "Holly Evans."

A Holly for Christmas. That's all I want.

"And you?" she asks with a swallow when I just stand there, openly staring at her in awe.

"Nate Thomas," I tell her. She nods her sweet head and drops her eyes to my hand that's gripping her arm a little too tight.

I catch myself and quickly release her even though every cell in my body is screaming at me to do the opposite—to grab on and never let go.

"Should we exchange information?" she asks as she glances back at her car. Her head turns and her big wooly scarf separates a few inches from her neck. I nearly buckle at the sight of her soft supple flesh underneath it. I want to put my lips on her skin as I strip her bare, revealing the rest of this angel's heavenly body. I want to see every inch of her. The gentle sloping curve of her hips, the round and plumpness of her young breasts, her sexy belly button, the arch of her spine, the light tuft of hair between her legs, the pinkness of her pussy as I slowly pry it apart with my fingers…

Fuck… Warm shivers overtake me as I think about what it would be like to have this girl naked in front of me, able to do whatever lewd and obscene things I want.

That would be a Christmas to remember. It would be my favorite one.

"Sir?" she says when I don't answer. It's getting hard to

talk with the way my heart is pounding and with the way my mind is obsessing over her.

I already know I'm fucked. This is so bad.

There's no way I'm letting this innocent little beauty escape. I'm not letting her go.

She's mine now and there's no going back.

"Yes," I say in a deep throaty voice. "Give me your information."

"My license?"

I swallow hard. "Yes."

Our cars didn't hit, so exchanging information is unnecessary, but I'll be damned if I'm going to give up the chance to get this sweet angel's address.

She pulls her license out of her pocket and hands it to me. I snap a picture of it with my phone, loving that I can now pull it up and stare at the tiny photo of her staring straight at the camera whenever I want.

She has nice long brown hair under that hat. I can't wait to get her inside and peel it off slowly, letting those soft gorgeous locks tumble down on her shoulders, on her neck, on my trembling hands.

My cock is coming to life despite the cold, getting hard and long as it strains against my pants. It aches with being so close to this dream girl, but at the same time, being so far away.

"And yours?" she says.

What the fuck is with me? I'm such a mess.

I reach into my jacket pocket and pull out my wallet. She pulls out her phone as I grab my driver's license and hand it to her.

"You're a doctor?" she asks when she reads it.

I nod. "A surgeon."

She looks impressed as she watches me.

I grin as she takes the photo. I've saved a lot of lives in my career, but seeing that look in her sexy eyes as she looked up at me was worth all the years of studying, the insanely long hours, the stress, the crazy high tuition, the intense pressure… It was all worth it for that moment. To see my girl looking up at me like I'm something special.

Holly keeps her phone out and starts thumbing through it. The blue light glows on her face, creating an ethereal look that's getting me lightheaded. She's so stunning. My body craves her in a bad way.

"What are you doing?" I ask with an edge to my voice.

If she's texting a boyfriend to come and get her, I don't know what the hell I'm going to do. I don't care if this little prick got to her first, she's mine now and I'm not giving her up for anyone or anything. I'll leave him on the side of the road if he tries to take her from me. The snow will bury him. The newspapers will wonder where he is. They'll find him in spring when the snow melts, beaten and bruised by my fists. That's what any man deserves for daring to touch what's mine. That's what they'll get if they try to take my Holly away.

"I'm trying to find a tow truck," she says as she scrolls on her phone. "Well, two tow trucks, I guess."

I put my hand over her screen and her shocked eyes dart up to mine.

"We don't need a tow truck," I tell her. "We don't need anyone."

She glances back over her shoulder and that spot of flesh on her slender neck becomes visible again, furiously tempting me. "But my car…"

"You're not driving that thing again."

Her eyes widen. "But it's not that badly damaged."

"You're not driving it," I repeat in a more forceful

voice. "It's unsafe. It's a wreck waiting to happen. I'm not letting you get into it again. You're too precious for a car like that."

She deserves a tank to bring her around. I want several thick inches of bulletproof metal around her, keeping her safe.

"But that's all I have."

"I'll buy you a new one," I tell her. "Any model you want."

Her shoulders drop as she looks up at me. She thinks I'm fucking with her. That I'm making fun of her. She's going to find out how serious I am. There's nothing this girl will want that I won't provide her. She'll see soon enough.

"I'm not joking, Holly," I tell her. "My sister and her husband own a dealership. I'll get you the latest safest SUV. Fully loaded with luxury. The works."

She looks so confused. "But why?"

I slip my glove off and gently graze my hand over her chin. "Because it's Christmas. You can think of me as your guardian angel. That's what I am now. I'll always be looking out for you, Holly Evans. I'll always be yours."

Our eyes connect for a long heated moment as the heavy flakes of snow float down around us. They cover our shoulders and stick to our jackets, making it feel like we're in a snow globe. Like we're in a dream. Everything about this encounter has felt like a dream.

"Let's get my truck out of the snow and we'll get out of here."

She glances back at her car. It's already buried in a fresh coat of snow. "What about mine?"

"Leave it here. I'll have it towed in spring. It's not safe enough for your priceless body."

She just watches me in shock and confusion as I head back to the truck.

"Hop in behind the wheel," I tell her. "You're going to have to steer while I push it out."

Her feet start moving under my command and she gets into my truck as I walk through the heavy snow to the front bumper.

I can't believe she's in my truck. That sweet ass is on my seat, her warm pussy close to the leather. Her hands grip my heated steering wheel, her divine face lit up from the lights in the dashboard. I have to take a moment to admire her like this before I get to work. My heart thumps in my chest as my cock groans in need.

"Put it into reverse and hit the gas," I call out to her as I bend down with a sigh and put my hands on the huge bumper. I'm jacked as fuck under this suit but I'm so shaky with nerves, excitement, and swelling emotion that I don't think I could push a shopping cart.

I brace my feet and bend down, ready to push when I hear the engine roaring.

My eyes dart up. I can't help myself. I steal another look at her. She looks so small behind the big wheel, hands gripping it as she watches me.

I smile at her and her cheeks turn pink as she smiles shyly back at me.

She truly is a Christmas miracle. Those Hallmark movies are starting to make a lot of sense.

The engine growls to life and the tires squeal as they spin in the snow.

With a grunt, I push the truck as hard as I can, every muscle in my body flexed to the max. The truck is stuck deep in the thickly packed snow, but I push and push until it starts to give. The tires get traction and the truck flies backward onto the road.

I fall to my knee and quickly get up when I see Holly in the driver's seat, pumping her fist with a big excited smile on her face. I nearly die. She's fucking perfect.

My hungry eyes never leave her as I walk over and open the door. "Hop over," I tell her as I climb inside. She climbs over the middle console and slips into the passenger's seat.

"Would you mind giving me a lift somewhere? I think there's a bus station nearby. If you don't mind."

A bus station. Like I would ever in a billion years drop this innocent little beauty off at a goddamn bus station.

"You're coming with me," I tell her as I grab the wheel.

"Where?"

My eyes focus on her soft plump lips. Her face is the poster child for angelic purity. I didn't think there was still pure innocence in the world, but here she is, staring back at me with those big blue eyes and changing my whole worldview.

"We're going to my brother's house," I tell her. "He's having a Christmas Eve party."

"Oh," she says, her eyes dropping to her hands. "And you want me to wait in the car?"

I try not to laugh. She's so sweet. It's not nice to laugh at her innocence. It's for admiring, treasuring, and worshipping. Not for laughing at.

"No, you're coming in with me," I tell her as I throw the truck into drive. "You're going to be my date."

"Your date?" she says with a gasp. "But I'm... I'm not dressed appropriately. I've been volunteering at the soup kitchen and I got most of it on my sweater."

Volunteering at a soup kitchen on Christmas Eve...

Does it get more virtuous and honest than that? She truly is an angel.

I don't deserve her. I'm not good like her.

All I can think about right now is defiling her. Claiming her. Taking that innocence as I sink my hard thick cock between her legs and discovering if her ripe little pussy is as soft as I'm dreaming it is.

She deserves the best, and I'm not the best. I'm a greedy bastard who takes what he wants.

And I want her.

So, even though I know I don't deserve her, I'm still not going to let her go.

Not ever.

I hit the gas and take her away.

She's my Christmas miracle and I'm keeping her.

If anyone disagrees, they can try and peel her from my strong, possessive hands.

Good luck.

CHAPTER THREE

Holly

My hands are folded on my lap as I stare forward in Nate's truck. The snow is still coming down hard, blurring the dark road as the big flakes fall.

I fidget with my jacket nervously as Nate plows forward, tearing through the fresh snow like my car was incapable of doing. My car that is now buried under a layer of thick snow somewhere on the side of the road. By morning, it's going to be completely inaccessible. I doubt I'll be able to get a tow truck until December twenty-seventh and by then, I'll be lucky if I can even find it.

I can feel Nate's presence radiating beside me. His hands are gripping the steering wheel so hard. His knuckles are white. It must be from the snow. He must be a nervous driver like I am.

I suck in a quick breath and glance at him. As soon as I turn, he does too. Our eyes meet and it sends a jolt of lightning through me, waking my body up. My back straightens in the seat, my hands fidget harder with my jacket, my heart pounds.

He's so sexy. Dark and mysterious in that alluring way that always gets me.

I lean back and steal a quick peek at him as he turns back to the windshield. His arms are so thick. This man pushed his truck out of the heavy snow with one push. He's so powerful. So strong. The unstoppable force of this man should be terrifying to me, but it's not. It's getting me all hot and bothered as I squirm in the seat.

It's a turn-on to be sitting here with him in his truck. I'd love to be wanted by a man like him. I can picture us heading out on a real date, me dressed up in fancy clothes, about to pull up to the latest hottest restaurant, feeling like a real woman, feeling like someone worth loving, knowing later that he's going to take me and love me in the way that only he can.

I get all warm and shivery just thinking about it.

"So, you're a surgeon?" I ask, trying to break some of the silence.

His hands clench on the steering wheel when he turns and looks at me with those dark smoldering eyes.

"I specialize in heart surgeries."

"Oh," I say, feeling way out of my league with this man. I barely make ends meet with my job as a daycare teacher. He must make in a week what I make in a year.

"I've studied hearts my entire life," he says as his voice gets raspier and sexier. "But I never understood them until now."

I stare at him in confusion. "What do you mean?"

He looks at me and takes a deep breath. "I understand what their function is. They're basically a pump that sends blood coursing around a body, providing oxygen and nutrients and carrying away waste. But I never got it. Never comprehended the significance of a heart until I met you."

I swallow hard as I stare at him. His eyes are focused on the road, thank god. I don't think I could handle them on me right now. Not with my body humming like this.

"Did I nearly give you a heart attack when I ran you off the road? Is that what you're talking about?"

"No," he says as his dark eyes roam all over me, leaving goosebumps in their wake. "That's not what I'm talking about at all."

"Then what?"

He pulls the car over to the side of the empty road and focuses those intense brown eyes onto me. I feel so small next to him. So vulnerable. But I like it. It's scary in an exciting way.

"When I saw you earlier," he says in a low controlled way, like he's making sure to say the perfect words. "I suddenly understood poems and love songs. I understood the true significance of a heart and all it represents."

The fat snowflakes land all over the truck, coating us in a layer of snow as we sit there. It feels like we're insulated in this truck from the outside world. Anything can happen in here. The air gets thick with need and want as we stare at each other unabashedly.

My concerns and worries about my car and where we're going and about this stranger of a man fall away as he looks at me. Strong desire and want take their place.

I'm drawn to this man. My body keeps inching closer to him—breath quickening, chest fluttering, heat flowing between my legs. I don't know what it is, but it's like my body knows something that I don't. Like it's recognized its other half and is trying to push me into his arms.

"You're stunning," he says as my mouth waters. "I never thought I'd find someone to drive me wild with desire, but when I saw you… I realized how wrong I've always been. You make me crazy, Holly. One look at you and I can feel the obsession taking over. It scares me."

I want to believe him, but what can he know about me after we've only met for ten minutes? We've barely talked.

My eyes drop down to my mittens. It would be like a Christmas movie if it were true—a real miracle over the holidays—but it's not. It's just… I don't know what it is…

"Let's just go," he says as he puts the truck back into drive. "We'll get into the warm house, put on some clean clothes, and then we'll see how you feel. Then, I'll make you understand."

I want to understand. I really do.

But I'm like the girl at the start of the holiday movie who doesn't quite believe in the magic of Christmas.

And no matter how hot and tempting this man is, he's not going to change my mind.

"This is a huge party," I say as we walk up to the enormous house. It's a gorgeous place with a three-car garage and a front lawn that you can play a game of pickup football on. Upbeat Christmas music is playing and there are beautiful lights and fun decorations everywhere I look. It's amazing.

"It's my brother's house," Nate says as he holds my hand. I wish we were in a warm place that didn't require gloves so I could feel his soft warm skin on mine. "He freaking *loves* Christmas."

"I can tell."

The door opens and a younger (but not as good looking) version of Nate steps out to grab a beer from the mountain of beer cases on the front porch.

"Hey!" he shouts with a big smile when he sees us. "Nate the Great! And who is this?"

"This is my girl," Nate says, proudly presenting me. "Holly Evans."

"Nice to meet you," I say politely.

"This is my brother, Tom," Nate says with a grin. "Don't be fooled by the big house. He's a total idiot."

Tom lets out a belly laugh. "Yeah, it runs in the family. Come on in, guys. Grab a drink! Warm up!"

I watch with my body tingling as Nate hugs his brother. This looks so fun. I can see people in dresses, suits, and ugly Christmas sweaters inside, dancing, laughing, drinking. It's the most festive party I've ever been to.

"Coming?" Nate says as he turns to me with a grin.

I nod and bound up the steps, excited to join in.

My excitement plummets when I step inside and see all of the fancy people in the gorgeous house. I'm not dressed for this. Not even close.

I have dried-up lentil soup all over my ugly sweater. It's not an ugly (but actually really cute) Christmas sweater like some of the guests are wearing. This sweater is just ugly. Full stop. It's the kind of sweater you wear when serving lentil soup at a soup kitchen. Not the kind you wear to a fancy Christmas party where you don't know anyone.

"Nate!" a pretty woman about my size says as she comes rushing over with her arms open. I'm surprised to feel a bit jealous as she gives him a big hug. "It's so good to see you!"

"Crystal," Nate says as he turns to me with a look of pride in his eyes. "This is my girl, Holly."

Her face lights up and she smacks his arm. "You didn't tell me you had a girl!"

She's suddenly playing with the tips of my hair as she looks me up and down with a big excited smile on her face. "Welcome to my house! I'm the sister-in-law. Tom's wife."

"It's a beautiful house," I say as I look around in awe. "So Christmasy."

"Thank you," she says with a gracious smile. She's so beautiful with long red curls in her hair and a sparkly silver dress. I want to be her when I grow up.

"Holly was volunteering at the soup kitchen," Nate says.

My cheeks heat up as she smiles extra wide. "That's so nice! What a sweetheart you are!"

"I picked her up from there," Nate continues, "and she forgot her change of clothes. Any chance you can lend her a dress for the evening?"

"No, that's okay," I quickly say, waving my hands in front of me. "I don't want to be a bother."

I would die if I got to try on one of those sparkly dresses or just be able to peek into Crystal's closet, but it's too much to ask. Her dress looks like it had way too many zeroes on the end of it to be lending out. I'd imagine the rest of her extravagant closet is the same.

"Nonsense!" she says with a big smile as she slides her arm over my shoulder and starts guiding me to the giant staircase. "I have a dark blue sparkling one that would light up your eyes. Yes! I want to see you in that one. Nate will freak!"

I glance over my shoulder at him as we start going up the stairs. He's watching me with those intense eyes as he peels off his jacket and hands it to his brother.

Wow... I didn't realize he was so muscular. His arms are round and hard under that suit. His chest is massive. I swallow hard when I see a sexy tattoo on the back of his hand. This man is full of surprises.

I'm excited to get a closer look at him without a jacket and gloves on, but Crystal is talking a mile a minute as she pulls me down the hall and into her room.

Her closet does not disappoint.

I gasp when she opens the double doors, revealing the rows and rows of stunning dresses and expensive shoes. It's bigger than my apartment in here.

She squeals in delight as she rushes over to a row of ballgowns and pulls out a shimmering dark blue one.

The light shines off the little crystals embedded into it, giving it a magical almost heavenly look. It's stunning. Something a movie star would strut down the red carpet in. I can't take my eyes off it.

"What do you think?" she asks as she holds it up.

I can't talk, so I just nod my head.

"I love it," I eventually manage to croak out. "I really, really love it."

She grins as she hands it to me. "And so will Nate!"

CHAPTER FOUR

Nate

"She's perfect," Tom says as he hands me a beer. "A little young, though, no?"

I glare at him as he opens his can of beer and it fizzes onto the carpet.

"Shit!" he says as he rubs it in with his shoe. "Crystal is going to kill me. If she asks tell her it was Jeff. She hates him anyway."

He takes a sip of his beer and looks around. "What were we talking about again?" he asks.

Gotta love my brother. He's a total idiot, but somehow makes it work for himself. While I was busting my ass in med school for a decade, he was smoking weed and playing video games. He must have cycled through two dozen jobs, all of them involving flipping something on a grill, and he sucked at all of them.

The lucky fuck bought two hundred dollars worth of

Bitcoin when it was only thirty-five cents a coin and now it's all getting close to being worth fifty million dollars. Talk about luck. He thinks he's a genius investor, but I know he's just got a lucky horseshoe wedged far up his ass.

All power to him. He's an idiot, but he's got a good heart and I still love him. I'm happy for his success.

"Oh, yeah," he says as he waves at someone I don't know. "A little young, no?"

I nearly growl at him. "She's my light," I tell him in a deep primal voice that shocks even me. "It doesn't matter what age she is. We're meant to be together."

"I didn't realize it was that serious," he says as his eyes dart around the room. The guy can't stand still and focus on a conversation with all this action around him. "I'm excited for you. Me and Crystal worry about you sometimes."

"You do?" I ask in a flat voice before taking a sip.

"Yeah," he says with a nod. "All you do is work and work and work. It's about time you get yourself a girl. Working sucks, man. Don't do it so much. Look at me. I've barely worked a day in my life and look at this place!"

"If I don't work as hard as I can, people die."

How many times do I have to explain this to him? He can't seem to get it into his thick skull that people and their families depend on my expertise. If I can't give it to them, or if I'm impaired in any way, their loved ones die. How can I not give my all with that on the line?

"People are always going to die, Nate," he says with a shrug.

"Not on my operating table. Not if I can help it. Do you have any idea how it feels to lose a patient on your watch. Because of something you did?"

Tom shakes his head. "No. I don't."

"And neither do I," I answer proudly. "Over seven hundred operations without one casualty. Well, technically there was one but it was because he fell down the stairs on the way out. Not my fault. It wasn't because of his heart. So, essentially zero."

"But you're the best heart surgeon in the country now, so you can relax a little and start to live or the first casualty will be your own life. You'll die a miserable old man who everyone hates."

"Oh really?" I say with a laugh.

He laughs too. "Oh yeah. Just like uncle Herb. Nyheim! That's my buddy from my Fortnite group. I gotta go say hi."

He takes off, but his words are still swirling around in my head. I have worked too hard for too long. I'm at the top of my game. It's time to take my hands of the accelerator and time to put them on my new angel.

A flash of sparkling blue catches my eye at the top of the stairs. I turn with a gasp when I see Holly walking down in slow motion.

Seriously. Time slows as she takes each step. This girl's beauty has broken time. It's broken me.

I'm standing here with my heart aching in my palm as she places her hand on the thick wooden banister and smiles at me.

She's utterly stunning. I've never seen anything like her.

That dress is incredible. I'm buying it off Crystal. That thing was made for my girl's body. It glides off her shoulders and travels down her slim arms, stopping at her wrists. It hugs the alluring curve of her hips and stops above her knees. Oh, those legs… I'm practically starting to pant as I imagine throwing those smooth legs over my shoulders and having her inner thighs digging into my ears as I get a taste of her sweetness.

Her brown hair is down and her gorgeous blue eyes are brighter than ever. She tucks a strand of her loose hair behind her ear as she smiles shyly at me. It makes me want her so badly. I can feel the hunger, the craving, the longing—all of it, eating away at me. I'm in agony as I stand here, watching her and struggling to control myself.

She has no idea how sexy she is. What a seductress she is. How she's tormenting me with every movement she makes. She's oblivious to it all.

That's what breaks me the most. She's completely unaware of the intense sexuality brimming all around her. How she drives men crazy with need. What she does to me. She's so damn innocent that she doesn't realize it.

It kills me that other men can see her like this. I get a shaking rage inside as I imagine them looking at her, putting their depraved and obscene eyes all over this angel. She's mine alone to look at. Mine alone to talk to. I'll kill anyone who has a problem with that.

She's also wearing some of Crystal's makeup. I loved Holly's face au natural, but she looks beautiful like this too. A bit of pink on her shiny lips, mascara to make her blue eyes pop even more, red blush on her cheeks or maybe that's just from knowing my hungry eyes are on her.

I don't stop staring at her as she walks down the staircase making a grand entrance into the party, making a grand entrance into my life.

I'm lightheaded and woozy by the time she walks up to me, hands clasped in front of her, shy smile on her breathtaking face.

"What do you think?" she asks as she bounces up on her toes. "Too much?"

My eyes ravish her up close. She's unbelievable. The curve of her little breasts are tempting me in a powerful way. I want to put my hands all over her. I want to kiss her. I want to do so many things, but thinking about them all is going to give me a massive hard-on in the middle of a party, so I try to focus on anything else.

"Everything about you is too much," I tell her in a desperate voice. "Your beauty, your allure, your innocence, the way it all comes so naturally to you. I feel overwhelmed in your presence. I want to know everything about you, but I can't think straight when you're looking at me with those big blue eyes. You're the most intriguing woman I've ever seen. You are stunning in that dress and I don't know how I'll ever be able to pull my eyes away from you."

She smiles shyly, those adorable cheeks turning a virtuous shade of pink. The things I'm going to do to her once I get her alone…

She'll never forget this night. It will be her favorite Christmas memory ever.

Fuck Santa. Fuck Christmas trees and gingerbread houses. Fuck waking up on Christmas morning and running down the hallway. Those favorite memories won't stand a chance after she's felt my cock deep inside her. I'll give her a new meaning of Christmas.

"Thank you," she says as she drops her eyes to the floor. "I feel a bit… too extravagant in it."

"You were extravagant when I saw you in the snow," I tell her. "You can't help but be extravagant. It's hopeless to fight it."

"Nate!" my cousin Sean shouts as he slaps a big hand

on my back. I tense up, wanting to bare my teeth and snarl at him like an animal for interrupting us. I finally found the girl for me and there's a party full of people trying to take my attention away from her. This is going to be much harder than I thought.

"Hey Sean," I grunt to him, although I don't take my eyes off my angel.

"Who is this?" he says slowly as he perks up and smooths out his hair. "I'm Sean. What's your name? I bet it's something beautiful."

He puts his hand out to Holly and I nearly grab it and snap his fingers in half. I'd like to, but I got to control this insatiable animal part of me if I don't want to ruin my brother's party. Instead, I slap his back hard, just like he did to me (only I didn't go flying forward like he does).

"This is my girl," I say, part words, part growl. "And I was just about to get her a drink."

I swallow her tiny hand in mine and pull her to the bar, possessiveness ripping through me. I want to *own* this girl. I want everyone to know it too. I want everyone to think one thing when they look at her: off-limits.

Of course Tom has a bar in his living room. There's no more Tom thing than that.

"What can I get you two lovebirds?" the bartender asks. She's a young blonde whose eyes linger on me as she runs her finger around the rim of the glass filled with maraschino cherries.

"Champagne?" I ask my new girl.

She nods. "Okay. I've never had it, but I've always wanted to try it."

The bartender grabs two glasses and fills them with some bubbly.

"Cheers," I say as I clink my glass to Holly's. "We're celebrating tonight. Our lives have changed forever."

"Oh, really?" She's grinning at me. "In what way?"

The bartender is eavesdropping. I don't want anyone to hear this next part but my girl.

"Come." I take her hand and guide her over to the huge Christmas tree. The thing is enormous. I have to tilt my head all the way back to see the top and even then I can't see the angel. My brother and his wife will spend their money on anything. If they're not more careful, Tom is going to be back to flipping burgers and asking me for money every month.

"This place is gorgeous," Holly says as she touches the tree. "I've never seen such a big tree in a house before."

"My brother loves Christmas," I repeat with a shrug as I stare at her. She's admiring the tree, that adorable chin tilted up, her sexy neck exposed in front of me. I groan from need when I see the lights reflecting in her blue eyes. She's lit up with the soft glow of it, giving her an ethereal almost magical look.

She wraps those sweet plump lips around her glass and takes a sip of the champagne. I smile as her nose twitches up when the bubbles tickle it.

"You were saying something about our lives changing?" she says as she looks up at me with those wide curious eyes. "I know how my life is going to change. I'm going to be taking the bus from now on." She covers her eyes with her hand and shakes her head. "I can't believe I lost my car. It's probably under ten feet of snow by now."

I take her wrist and gently pull her hand away from her face. "I'm going to take care of it. I promise. I'm taking care of you now, Holly. I'm taking care of all of your needs. *All* of them."

Those sexy little lips part as her eyes roam down to my big shoulders and then over my arms. I hope she likes tattoos because my arms and chest are covered in them.

"Tell me about yourself," I beg. "I want to know it all. Every fascinating detail."

"It's not too fascinating," she says shyly. If only she knew how absolutely captivating I find her. She doesn't see her true value. "I'm a daycare teacher."

"You take care of kids all day?"

She smiles and nods. I can see that. There's a sweet gentleness to her that kids would respond well to. I can't wait to see her with our kids. I'm going to give her as many as she can handle. I can't wait to get started breeding that ripe budding womb. I groan from thinking about it.

"I do," she continues in that soft lyrical voice. "I know most adults find it boring, talking to kids, making crafts, singing silly songs all day, but I don't know… It's fun. It's very rewarding."

She catches herself and drops her eyes. "Not as rewarding as saving lives like you, obviously…"

"It is," I say as I take her hand and get those stunning blue eyes back onto me. "You are saving lives. A lot of those kids can't get a second of attention from their parents. All they see is them staring at their phones. You give it to them. You're a light in their day, like you're a light in mine. Their spirits would be broken if it wasn't for you."

"I wouldn't go that far," she says with her cheeks turning pink.

"I would."

We look at each other for a long heated moment, our

eyes locked on one another. I step closer and a quiver teases through her as those sweet lips part.

I'm going to kiss her. I need to taste her soft mouth. I want to consume her breath and steal her sweetness.

Her chin tilts up and her eyes fall closed as I cup her jaw with my hand, my eyes locked on her mouth. She's so gorgeous all sparkly and Christmasy. Holding champagne next to the lit-up tree. I feel like I've stepped into a damn dream.

I take a second to admire her before diving in, about to seal my lips to hers.

"Nate!"

I yank my head to the side and see my older sister and her husband approaching with her arms wide open, big smile on her face.

Fuck. Worst possible timing.

Holly's eyes snap open and she turns to Sandy, looking a little unsteady. She was wanting the kiss as much as I was.

"Tom said you were here with a girl and I just had to see it with my own eyes!" Sandy hugs me and rests her hand on my arm. "Are you trembling? Why are you shaking like this?"

I haven't stopped shaking since I met this angel. She belongs on the top of the tree.

"I'm fine," I grunt. "This is my girl, Holly. Holly, this is my sister, Sandy, and her husband, Doug."

They all shake hands and I have to fight back a growl when I see Doug's hand sliding into Holly's. He's been family for over a decade, but I still don't like seeing them touch. I guess I'm a possessive fucker like that.

"I *love* that dress," Sandy says as she looks Holly up and down. Doug's eyes are about to follow his wife's, but I clear my throat and give him a warning look. He understands immediately that this girl is not to be gawked at.

"I'm going to go freshen up my drink," he says before quickly fleeing. Good move. Doug was always a smart one.

"How did you two meet?" Sandy asks.

"Holly came *crashing* into my life at the perfect time," I say with a grin. "I didn't know what hit me."

She giggles and my heart nearly collapses in on itself.

"So, has it been long?" Sandy always wants all the details. Every family has a gossiper and she's ours.

"It's felt like a lifetime," I say as I take my girl's hand. "It feels like I've known this beauty forever."

"And it feels like I've been waiting for this man my entire life," she says as she puts her palm on my back, rubbing it. My eyes close. My brain stops functioning with her hands on me. "But he's here now. We're making up for lost time."

"How's the dealership going?" I ask Sandy. Her and Doug own a luxury car dealership in town. They do very well. I don't care about anything except getting to know my girl right now, but I want to change the subject off of us. If Sandy finds out that we just met an hour ago, she's going to tell everyone at this damn party.

"Fine, fine," she says, waving dismissively at me. "Back to you two. Where are you from, Holly?"

I look at her, wanting to know the same thing. *I* should be asking these questions, not my nosy sister.

"I'm from here," she says. "I live in town."

"Oh." Sandy nods. "And do you go to school? College or… high school?"

I glare at her. "She's an adult, Sandy. Geez. She's… how old are you?"

"Twenty-two."

"She's twenty-two."

"It's just that…" Sandy starts to mutter. "You're over forty now…"

"Okay, that's enough of that." I grab my girl's hand and bring her out of there. Why can't they understand that love knows no age? That I would die for this woman? That I would kill for her?

I clutch onto her hand in a possessive grip as I lead her through the party past Crystal's colleagues at the hair salon. She's tried to set me up with all of them, but I said no to each one. I didn't know it then, but I was waiting for Holly. My heart must have known it, even if I didn't.

"Where are we going?" she asks as we hurry down the hallway past the door that leads into the garage.

"Down here," I say as I open a door that leads to the basement. It's not a crappy basement like you'd find in most houses. Tom has a full-on man-cave down here. Huge bar, pool table, two bowling lanes, a fifty thousand dollar gaming station, enough TVs to watch all Sunday football games at once. The only thing this house is missing is a library. There's not a book in sight.

"Wow," she says as she looks around in awe. "Was this house designed by a teenage boy?"

I laugh. "It was designed by my brother, so basically, yeah. He's like a fourteen-year-old trapped in a man's body."

I'm still gripping her hand as we hurry past it all. Some of his gaming buddies are in front of the big TV, playing some stupid game and being loud about it. We're headed in the opposite direction.

I turn the corner and open the double wooden doors to Tom's wine cellar.

Holly gasps. "That's a lot of... beer?"

My brother really makes me laugh. He has a gorgeous five-thousand bottle wine cellar, but he doesn't like wine, so he's filled the shelves with bottles and cans of beer instead. He's a character.

"My brother is one of a kind," I say as I close the double doors and lock them.

Holly spins and looks at me with excitement in those blue eyes when she hears the click.

We're all alone now. It's nice and romantic in here. Quiet with soft lighting on the walls, casting us in a sensual glow.

We can do anything we want in here. I can do anything I want to her.

My cock hardens as I step forward and take my girl in my arms.

Right where she belongs...

CHAPTER FIVE

Nate

Desire and lust stir within me now that I have this girl all alone. There's not a pure thought in sight as I roam my hungry eyes over her, admiring every beautiful inch.

She's coming home with me tonight. I've decided it.

I still haven't decided if I'll ever let her leave. I don't think I'll be able to. The thought of this innocent little beauty in the world without my protective eyes watching out for her makes me all scratchy inside. It gives me an edgy feeling from just imagining it. I know I won't be able to handle it in real life.

"This is a great party," she says as she looks around shyly. Her cheeks are all rosy pink and that adorable color is making me ache with need.

I need her so badly. I hope she's ready for it. When I let loose, she's going to have a lifetime of arousal unloaded on her at once. I hope she can handle it. I hope my girl is as strong as I know she can be.

"My brother knows how to throw a party," I say with a croak in my voice.

"It's a great house for a party," she says as she places her empty champagne glass on the high round table. "Lot's of places for lovers to sneak off to."

"Like here?"

She swallows hard as she looks at me under her long lashes, those blue eyes smoldering with something hot. "Yeah. Like in here."

I step up to her and drag a lock of hair off her neck. "I want you."

She quivers as her eyes move to my lips. "You do?"

I nod. My hands slide down to her arms, but I have to be careful. The intensity of my need is dangerously high. I'm too strong for a delicate body like hers. I can squeeze her too hard or be too rough without even noticing. I have to focus on keeping my control in check.

"I do want you," I tell her, baring my soul to my soul mate. "But I want more than that. It runs deeper. I want you to want me."

Her mouth opens as those sexy blue eyes burn into me.

"I want you to want me like I want you. Like your soul will wither and die if you're not in my arms. I want you to *need* me. To *crave* me. I want you as obsessed with me as I am with you."

I must look so desperate with my longing for her, but I don't care. My pride is shadowed by my need to have her. It's all I care about.

"I do," she whispers softly. "I want you like that. I always will."

That's all the invitation I need.

Those alluring blue eyes widen as I wrap my arms around her and pull her against me. "Oh, Nate," she whispers as her mouth gravitates toward mine, her eyes closing on their own.

My lips come down on hers, rough and hard as I claim her mouth. She moans on my tongue as I taste her sugary innocence. Her hands slide up my back and those perky little tits press into my chest as I kiss her deeper.

I'm so fucking hard. My cock is stiff as a rock and longer than ever.

My Holly moans when I press it against her stomach. The shockwaves surge from my cock into my core and I shudder with pleasure.

"I'm so hard for you," I groan between wet kisses.

She's making these little whimpering sounds that make my cock jolt.

"I can feel it," she moans back. "You're making me so *wet*."

My jaw clenches as I pull away and look down at her. Knowing her pussy is soaked and waiting for me is too much to handle. My control snaps.

Suddenly, I'm turning her in my powerful hands and pushing her against the table.

She gasps as her palms land hard on the table, her ass thrust in the air. That sexy blue dress creeps up the back of her soft thighs as I drop to a knee while my heart pounds viciously in my chest.

Her curvy ass is right in front of my face. My mouth waters as I drag my hands up her legs, from her strappy high heels, over her calves, behind her knees, up her soft warm thighs. The warmth turns to heat the higher I go.

"You're going to learn quickly that if you try to tease

me with your pussy, you're going to have a mad man on your hands."

She looks at me over her shoulder with a grin. She batts those sexy eyelashes, like she's challenging me. "I'm *so* wet," she moans.

Fuck… She's trying to kill me.

She's swaying her sexy ass in front of my face, making my mouth water, making me pant.

I slide my fingers along the edge of her dress and slowly peel it over her ass, staring at her wet mound covered only by a thin layer of black lacy panties.

Her beautiful cheeks are covered in goosebumps right in front of my ravenous eyes. She's got a great ass. It's magnificent just like the rest of her.

"Let see how wet I make you," I say as I grab her panties and slowly pull them down.

Her legs start trembling as I bring them lower. "Fuck," I whisper when they slide past her little puckered asshole. My heart stops as I stare at it, mouth salivating like a beast. I'll fuck that tight little hole one day.

But for now, I'm focused on one place. One wet, warm, tight little place.

"*Oh*," she whines as I tug down and the lacy fabric peels off her pussy lips. She's so wet that a trail of her juices sticks to the panties as I slide them down her thighs.

"Spread your legs, angel. I want to get a good look at your pussy."

She steps to the side, the panties stretching tight around her knees, and sticks her ass out so her man can have a better look at what she's been keeping safe for him.

I nearly pass out at the sight waiting for me.

Her pussy is a dream. It's *beautiful*. Captivating me in every way.

I can't take my eyes off it as my heart pounds. My grip tightens on her thighs. I lick my lips as I stare up at it.

It's sparkly wet, her juices coating her swollen lips, an engorged little clit popping out of the top.

And that smell... *Mmmmmm*... Warm sugar.

She gasps as I touch her with both thumbs and gently pry those soft lips apart, revealing the virgin pink inside.

She's got to be a virgin. This pussy looks virgin tight, she's got that virgin innocent way about her, but most of all… She has to be. I won't be able to handle it if some fucking punk got here before I did. If he saw what I was seeing, tasted what I'm about to taste, claimed what's my birthright to claim. I'm getting all amped up and furious just thinking about it. I can feel my hands wrapping tightly around his neck as I squeeze out his last pathetic breaths.

"Tell me, Holly," I say in a raspy voice that's like sandpaper in my throat. "Tell me if I'm the first to see you like this."

Her cheeks are all red as she looks down at me. She's breathing heavily, her eyes with a lustful shine. "You are," she says with a moan. "I've never been with anyone. You're the first one to see this part of me."

Goddamn…

I'm dying over here.

"I haven't even had a kiss," she says. "I know it's crazy."

She's been saving herself for me. Keeping this cherry tight for me. Keeping her lips pure for me.

I'll never take that for granted. I'll never take her for granted. I'll treasure her forever.

Not even a kiss…

Her words save me. *She* saves me.

The anger melts away, replaced by an enormous sense of gratitude and a feeling of love. Of course she's untouched. Why did I even doubt it? An angel like her always has her innocence intact. But not for long… I'm hungry for it.

I slide my hands up to her bare ass and grip her cheeks hard. She whimpers as I dive in with a growl, devouring her cunt with my ravenous mouth and greedy tongue.

She cries out as I bury my mouth between her legs, digging my tongue into that tight little hole. The sensations are too intense and she tries to squirm away, but I wrap my powerful arms around her thighs and hold her against my mouth. Now that I have her, she's not going anywhere.

I'm a beast for her. I'm insatiable. I'm in heaven as I suck down every warm drop of cream she gives me.

It's a wet lovely mess as I slide my tongue through her folds and up to her clit. I wrap my lips around it and suck hard. She nearly buckles in my arms, but I'm holding her up, holding this sweet wet pussy to my hungry mouth.

She starts crying out more and more as I play with her clit. I flick and circle it with my tongue before sucking on it again. Her hips start moving to the rhythm of my tongue, gyrating on me as she starts humping my mouth, desperate to get off.

"Oh fuck, Nathan," she moans heavily. "I wasn't expecting this. How are you making me feel so good?"

I grin as she drops her head and takes a few quick breaths, her hands gripping the table hard. The sound of my full name on her lips nearly makes me unravel. Nobody calls me Nathan, but I like it from her. I could certainly get used to hearing it on her soft plump lips.

I slide a finger inside her, testing her out, and her pussy

clamps down hard around it. She's impossibly tight. I groan as I feel the compression of her silky tunnel trying to choke my finger out. She's perfect. I can't wait to break this virgin cunt in.

I'm taking her *raw*. I'm going to *breed* her ripe little womb, but first, I want her to cum all over my mouth.

My grip tightens on her thighs as I slide my finger out and replace it with my mouth. I eat her out in a frenzy. I devour her. I lick and suck and stroke her with my tongue like I'm a starved man. She cries out and grips the table until it's shaking as much as she is.

Her legs are trembling around me, her pussy getting wetter and hotter on my lips. My mouth is *everywhere*.

I'm desperate to get her off. I'm lusting to feel her cumming hard all over me.

It's all I can think about. It's all I want.

She cries out in shock and pleasure as I drag my tongue between her cheeks and tongue her adorable little asshole.

Her body shakes. It bucks against my face as I trace her hole with the tip of my tongue and then run it over her.

Fuck, I can't get enough of this girl.

I move back down to her pussy and groan when I find it wetter than ever.

"It's time for you to cum," I growl between licks.

She gasps as a quiver rips through her.

"I want to feel your hot pussy cumming all over my mouth," I groan. "Cum on me, Holly. Give me what I really want for Christmas—your virgin cream. Give it to me. *Now*."

She throws her head back, that long brown hair slapping her skin, and cries out.

Yes… I clutch onto her legs, press my mouth against her pussy lips, and moan as I feel her cumming hard.

Warm juice pours out and coats the lower half of my face—my lips, my chin, my tongue. It's everywhere and so fucking good.

It's the first time she's cumming on a man. My face first, my cock next. I want to see her cumming in every position in every way possible.

I lick her through her orgasm, loving the cute little whimpers she's making as she tries to stay quiet. Eventually, it becomes too sensitive for her and she pushes me away. Literally. She puts her hand on my face and pushes. I smile as I release her.

"I'm sorry," she says as her eyes squeeze closed. "It's so intense…"

"I know, angel," I say as I get up, dragging my hand over the curve of her bare ass. "You did so good though. You are truly delicious."

She pulls her dress back down with a wiggle as I stand up behind her. My hands are on her hips as she turns around and looks into my eyes.

"Kiss me," she begs.

"You want to taste how sweet you are?"

She nods, those sexy blue eyes driving me mad. "Yes."

I kiss her hard, thrusting my tongue into her mouth so she can taste what I tasted, so she can see how perfect she is.

She moans as I explore her mouth, sliding my tongue against hers as I add some pressure.

I nearly pass out when we pull away and she licks her lips. "Tasty."

"I told you."

Her eyes slowly move down my body as I hold her. They travel over my chest, down my stomach, to the hard outline of my erection jutting out of my pants like I have a damn baseball bat in my pocket.

Her mischievous hand follows her eyes, sliding from my arm all the way down to my cock.

I groan as she drags her palm along my shaft, nearly making me cum with one touch.

It's already a wet mess down there. I don't know how much pre-cum leaked out while I was sucking on her hot cunt, but it's a lot. My balls are aching with a huge load that's destined for her fresh womb.

Her eyes pop back up to mine as her hand explores my length. She looks so damn pure, it kills me. These big blue eyes with long dark lashes looking at me like she doesn't know what to do, but wants to learn.

"I want to do that to you," she says as she runs that hand up and down, up and down, mesmerizing me, killing me, torturing me. If I don't get some kind of release, I'm going to explode. My heart will stop. "I want to make you feel as good as you made me."

"You're already doing that, angel. I can't believe you're here in my arms. I've never felt this good in my life."

"But you can always feel better," she says as she bites that plump bottom lip, looking so sexy I could pass out. "There's always another level of pleasure."

I swallow hard as she drops to her knees. Her radiant blue eyes are locked on mine as she drags her hand all over my hard dick.

"*Fuck*," I groan as she drops her eyes to my belt and begins to thread the leather through the buckle.

She opens it and pulls down my zipper. My pants slide down my legs and bunch at my feet.

With her hands on my muscular thighs, she drags her tongue up my length, my boxer briefs the only thing separating her warm tongue from my burning flesh. She giggles and then reaches for my waistband.

I can't take my eyes off her as she peels them down and releases my cock. It springs up, hard and wet in front of her.

Her greedy little hand wraps around it and she stares at it in awe, her eyes getting that lustful glassy look to them. She squeezes my shaft and a bead of pre-cum oozes out of the slit on my head. She licks her lips and then brings it to her mouth.

My heart stops in my chest as I watch her pink tongue slip out and she licks my swollen head clean. "Mmmmm," she moans, eyes falling closed as she tastes me. "You taste even better than I do."

"Not possible," I say as I slide my hands into her hair. She lets me guide her mouth back to where it belongs. "Open wide."

She does as I say, parting those lips as she takes me into her mouth. My head drops back and my eyes close when I feel her soft lips wrap around me. Her tongue is sliding up my throbbing shaft, her hand clutching the thick base, the side of her hand pressing against my aching balls.

I force my eyes back open and look down, not wanting to miss a second of this. She starts sucking my cock as I drag her hair back to get a better view of her lips wrapped around me. It's a beautiful sight and the feeling is even better. It's earthshaking. It's life-changing. We're going to be touching each other in this beautiful way for the rest of our lives.

"You're so big," she gasps as she pulls my cock out to take a breath. She's still squeezing my shaft and staring at my dick with a mesmerized look on her face. Her little tongue slips out and I watch as she drags it around my dick, coating me in her sweet saliva.

"That's my girl," I growl as my grip tightens on her head. "Put it back in your mouth, baby. Suck on it hard."

She jumps back on it, sucking me like she's desperate to get me off. The feel of my dick brushing against the roof of her mouth, the length of her tongue, the back of her molars… fucking hell… I'm going to blow.

"Yes," I hiss through gritted teeth. "Don't stop. Don't stop…"

She bobs her head back and forth, running her tight lips along me as she squeezes the base of my shaft as hard as she can.

God, that fucking view… Her legs are spread, that sexy dress hitched high on her soft thighs. Her small tits hidden and waiting for me to explore. Her hair bobbing. Her mouth moving along my thick shaft.

I can't take it…

…and I fucking blow.

I grit my teeth and holler as I release in her mouth, cumming harder than I've ever cum before. My whole body flexes. It's tight all over and then… loose as thick streams of cum shoot out all over the back of my girl's mouth. I coat her tongue and the roof of her mouth with my hot load.

She whimpers when she feels it, hot and sticky in her mouth.

"Swallow it down, Holly. It belongs inside you."

Those innocent blue eyes are back on mine, big as ever while she swallows my load. I watch in awe—the intense orgasm tearing through me like a hurricane—as she licks her lips clean.

"Show me," I beg.

She opens up wide and shows me her tongue. It's clean. Just pink. All of my cream is sliding down her throat.

That should buy us some time.

I want to take this girl's cherry as soon as possible, but I'm not going to take it in a beer cellar with a bunch of man-child gamers outside. Not going to happen.

This angel deserves the best. She deserves a quiet empty house and a nice big bed. A roaring fire, soft sheets, and a man who's going to treat her right.

Later tonight, she'll get it all.

She'll get it right.

And she'll get it *hard*.

CHAPTER SIX

Holly

"After my wife gave birth," an older man is telling me. I think it's Nate's uncle, but I'm not sure. "I pulled the doctor aside and asked him, 'How soon until we can have sex?'"

I stare at him blankly.

"He winked at me and said, 'My break is in ten minutes. Meet me in the parking lot!'"

"Oooh!" I say as I point at him. He bursts out laughing, a deep hearty laugh that I'm worried is going to give him a stroke. His face turns bright red, but he's going to be fine.

I missed this. Bad jokes at family parties, fun appetizers, getting to know all sorts of people. To be honest, I was worried I wouldn't ever experience it again.

"So, tell me about your daycare," the woman beside him, Kathleen, asks me. "Are the kids just the cutest ever?"

"They are," I say with a smile. "Especially around

Christmas. They get so excited. There's true magic in the air."

There's true Christmas magic in the air here as well.

I look across the room and spot Nathan by the fireplace talking to his sister in hushed tones. His eyes dart to mine and I get that quivery feeling that is becoming all too familiar.

He's never taken me out of his sight. His eyes are constantly following me around the room like he can't get enough of me. My new man seems to be the obsessive type and his new obsession is me. How did I get so lucky?

I can still feel his mouth between my legs. It's glowing with heat down there. The pleasure hasn't gone away.

The older man begins to tell me another joke about a singing frog, but I tune him out and focus on my Christmas surprise. He's so hot. He's the best-dressed person here in a navy blue suit and white shirt. His tie is a little darker with small white polka dots.

I'm practically salivating as I watch him. He's all muscle under that fitted custom suit, looking like a Christmas present I'm desperate to unwrap. I want to peel back the layers and see what his wide chest looks like, see what his big arms feel like. I want to lick his abs and drag my hands over his round shoulders.

I love his style. I can't wait to see his other outfits… the casual look, Sunday football look, gym gear, pajama parties, and of course, in a bathing suit. I can't wait to see it all. Hopefully, by this time next Christmas, I will have.

It's not just his clothes and his perfectly sculpted body… His face is the type you can sit in front of for hours, lit up by candlelight, and never get bored as you stare at it. There are endless sights to see from his dark eyebrows that make his brown eyes shine brighter, to his stately nose and strong jawline. His mouth is a wonder, with his soft sexy lips and his straight white teeth. I can't get enough of him.

Nathan's uncle is back at it again. "I told my wife that her underwear is too tight and revealing."

She rolls her eyes as he giggles like a schoolchild.

"She told me to stop wearing it then."

He lets out another booming laugh as I smile politely.

"Oh, there's Mack and Linda!" Kathleen says when an older couple walks into the house. "Those are Nate's parents. Have you met them yet?"

I shake my head as I swallow nervously. They look friendly enough, smiling and laughing as Tom and Crystal greet them with hugs.

I don't know why I'm so nervous. I guess it's because I want them to like me. I want to be part of the family.

Nathan arrives back at my side and slips his hand over mine. "Sorry, I just had to deal with something with Sandy."

"Everything okay?" I ask as I look up at him. Those eyes are so beautiful as they reflect the lights of the Christmas tree.

"Everything is great." He gives my hand a squeeze and then starts pulling me. "Come. I want to introduce you to my parents."

His parents already? I gulp as I head over. I guess this is the real deal.

"Mom, Dad," he says as he presents me. "Let me introduce you to the girl I'm going to marry."

"Oh," his mother says, doing a double-take as she looks at me. "So, nice to meet you. And what is my future daughter-in-law's name?"

"I'm Holly," I say with a shy smile.

"A Christmas Holly," his dad says with a big warm smile. "How fitting. I'm Mack and this is Linda. We can't wait to meet you and hear all about our son's first serious relationship. But I really need a stiff drink to ease these old aching bones."

Tom returns with two drinks—a scotch for Mack and a glass of white wine for Linda.

"That's better," Mack says as he takes a sip.

"Come," Linda says as she wraps her arm around mine, already making me feel like I'm part of the family. "I want to hear *everything*."

I glance back at Nathan as she leads me into the kitchen, smiling and saying hello to people as we walk through the crowd. He smiles peacefully at me, looking like everything has fallen into place. I smile back, agreeing completely.

∼

"Everyone was so nice," I say, feeling full of energy like I can run alongside Nathan's moving truck. "Your brother and sister seemed a little unsure of the age difference but I think I was growing on them by the end of the party."

"They loved you," Nathan says as he glances at me with a smile. "Of course they did. How could they not?"

I talked to each of them for a while and I think they understood that I'm the one for Nathan and it really doesn't matter what year I was born in. All that matters is we're in love. I think they saw that too. They both said they've never seen their brother look so happy before.

"And your mom and dad are great! It was just..."

"What?" His forehead scrunches up in concern, but it's nothing like that.

"It was just so nice to be around a family during the holidays. I don't have that."

"You don't have *any* family?"

I tell him about my dad dying and never knowing my mom. "My brother is off somewhere in Asia," I say with a sigh. "I have no idea where. I'm not even sure if I'll ever see him again."

"You're all on your own?"

I nod, feeling tears well up.

He puts his hand on mine and I instantly feel better.

"Not anymore," he says and I almost believe him with the sincere way he's looking at me. "You're part of the family now. I'll be making it official before next Christmas."

"Oh, really?" I say in a flirty way. "Don't *I* get a say in the matter?"

"I don't think so," he says with a grin. "You're mine and I'm keeping you forever. I've decided it. That's what you get for almost killing me."

"If I knew that," I say as I innocently bat my eyelashes at him. "I would have tried to kill you a long time ago."

Our eyes lock on each other, but he eventually has to pull them away to look back at the road. The snow is still coming down hard.

We pass a huge familiar-shaped lump beside the road and I shake my head. "I'm never getting my car out of that."

"You won't need to," he says. "Santa might bring you some new wheels tonight."

I laugh. "I think a new car is too much even for Santa."

"But it's not for me." He grins as he flashes those sexy dark eyes at me.

"You're all the Christmas present I need," I tell him. "I can't believe this is happening. It's like a dream."

"You're a dream," he says. "One that I don't want to wake up from."

I smile as I wrap my hands around his and rest my head on his arm, wine and love flowing through my veins, making everything feel so damn perfect.

"Oh!" I say, perking back up after a few minutes of comfortable silence with my new man. "I forgot to give you my address. We just passed the exit."

"You really think I'm going to let you go home?" he asks with a mischievous grin on his handsome face.

"I was hoping you weren't."

He licks his lips and squeezes the steering wheel. "Good. Because you're coming home with me."

CHAPTER SEVEN

Holly

"This is your house?" I ask with my mouth hanging open when Nate plows into the snow-filled driveway. It's huge.

"I hope you like it," he says as he taps the button on the visor over my head and one of the four garage doors starts to open.

"I don't even know what to say. It's incredible."

"I did it all for you."

"What do you mean?"

His eyes get a softness to them that I haven't seen yet. It makes my heart warm up.

"All the studying, the work, getting up every day, and making all that money," he says as he looks at me. "I felt a drive pushing me. Now I know it was all for you. There's a reason why I'm nearly twenty years older than you, Holly. It's so I would have time to get our life ready for when you showed up. I could have the perfect house, on the perfect street, to give you the lifestyle you deserve. Now that you're here, all of my work, everything I've collected and earned over the years, it means something. I'm thrilled I get to share it with you."

I'm speechless as he pulls into the garage and the door closes behind us.

Even his garage looks rich. It's enormous with two more vehicles—a two-seater Porsche convertible and a motorcycle that looks insanely fast. I already know that I'm going to have a problem with him taking that bike out. I'm as protective as him as he is of me and I don't want anything to happen to him. What if another careless twenty-two-year-old girl swerves off the road and takes him out on that thing? I could never go on without him in my life.

"Nathan," I say softly. "I wish I could have been with you the entire time. Helping you, supporting you, encouraging you all along."

"You were," he says as he shuts off the car and turns in his seat, watching me with those sexy brown eyes. "I could always feel your presence."

"You could?"

He nods. "I knew you were out there waiting for me. All I had to do was find you."

"I'm glad you waited and that another girl didn't snatch you up."

He smiles. "It would never happen."

"But there must have been other women," I say, feeling my stomach drop. "A rich, single surgeon… You're quite the catch. I bet you had women lining up around the hospital waiting for you to get off your shift."

I smile, but I don't feel it. I'm feeling sick just thinking about him with another woman. With his arms around her, his lips kissing hers. I suck in a breath as I try to hold back tears. I really don't want to ruin this moment by sobbing in his car.

"I told you, I waited," he says and my heart starts to lift back up. "I was waiting to find you."

"Does that mean?" It can't…

He nods. "I'm a virgin too, Holly. Your lips were the first ones to be wrapped around my cock and the first lips to touch mine."

Relief fills me as my heart drums in exhilaration. I'm his first? I was hoping, but not crazy enough to believe it.

It all clicks into place now.

We are soul mates. I thought I recognized it when I first saw him in the snow, but now I know it's true. We're made for each other.

That's why no other boys or men could hold any interest from me for long. That's why I'm so drawn to him.

His family will be my family one day. My kids will be able to grow up experiencing a full Christmas. A Christmas full of family, full of love, full of magic.

They'll grow up knowing that their parents were made for one another and meant to be together. Forever.

We both lean in and our lips connect in a soft loving kiss that has me moaning and reaching for him. I want to feel his big hard body pressed against me once again. I want to feel those possessive arms holding me, making me certain I'm his. I want to feel that thick cock—hard and begging for my body—digging into my thigh.

"Come sit on Santa's lap," he says as he grabs me and pulls me onto him. I moan as I straddle his big frame, ducking my head to stop it from hitting the roof of his truck.

My dress hikes up my thighs and he looks down at my panties that are barely covering my aching pussy. It's my first time wearing sexy lacy underwear. Crystal lent them to me. I didn't want to take them at first, but she laughed and said that if I'm wearing this dress, I'm going to need sexy underwear underneath.

"You're like a Christmas present ready to be unwrapped," she said as she shoved a bra and panties into my chest. "The real gift is underneath. Put it on. Trust me, you won't regret it."

What can I say? She was right.

Although, she won't be too happy to get them back with what I'm doing to them. They're all wet.

I don't know if I'll ever be able to wear a dry pair of underwear again with this sexy man in my life.

His strong hands grip my ass as I lean down and kiss him. My hips move to the rhythm of his tongue and he groans as I start grinding against his erection.

It sends jolts of pleasure and euphoria ripping through me as I grind my spread pussy up and down his length.

"Fuck," I whimper between kisses as his big hands travel up to my breasts. He grabs them firmly over my dress as he nibbles on my bottom lip.

My hips don't stop. I'm gyrating faster and harder, jerking his dick off with my hot pussy.

The pressure builds within, until I can't take it anymore and it snaps.

I scream out and throw my head back, smacking it on the roof as another orgasm hits.

Nathan grabs the back of my neck and holds my open gasping mouth to his as I cum hard. "Yes," he growls, his warm breath tickling my lips. "I love it when your pussy cums. Don't stop grinding on me. Get those sweet juices all over my dick."

I do as he says and grind on him some more as the orgasm fades and a trembling takes its place. I'm so wet now. My pussy juices have leaked through my panties and made a mess all over his pants. I don't think he's going to care one bit.

"You're so fucking sexy," he growls against my mouth as my hips slow. My blood feels thicker, like I can barely move. "I want you in my bed where I can take my time unwrapping you. I still haven't seen these beautiful tits."

I suck in a breath and hold it as his hungry eyes drop down to my chest. My nipples are so hard. It feels like they've been aching all night for him.

A few minutes later, I manage to pry my cramping leg off him and we head into the house.

It blows my fucking mind. I don't know what I was expecting from the outside, but the inside has blown away every expectation I had.

It's insane.

Chef Ramsay would cream his pants if he saw Nathan's kitchen. The island is the biggest island I've ever seen. Probably bigger than Iceland. Not literally, but you get the point. He has a gas stove that I could fit in and a long dining room table that could fit his entire family, plus some.

The expensive art on the walls, the big comfy couches, the enormous stone fireplace, the view...

I'm in heaven.

He even has a huge Christmas tree decorated. So cute.

"Look around," he says as he peels off his jacket and starts to unbutton his sleeves. "Make yourself at home. Because you are home."

I swallow hard as I watch him roll his sleeves up his thick tattooed forearms. He's so freaking sexy. I had no idea he had so many tattoos until now, but they suit him. I should have known that he would be all inked up.

The house is the type you can get lost in for hours, everywhere you look something to catch your attention—but my attention is locked on Nathan.

He leans down, grabs some firewood from the pile, and opens the glass fireplace doors. I grin, picturing him shirtless in the fall, red and yellow leaves tumbling down all around him, as he chops wood with those big sexy arms. Grunting like a real man as I watch all bundled up in a wool sweater, hot cocoa in my hands. That's an image to look forward to. It's only going to be about ten months away. I can't wait.

My eyes are all over his back as he stacks the logs in the fireplace and adds some newspaper. Excitement builds within me, knowing how romantic this softly lit room is going to be once he lights that match.

I'm tingling all over as he strikes it and a flame appears. My eyes wander to his muscular thighs as he leans down and lights the fire.

It catches and a warm glow fills the big room. I'm already warm and I'm already glowing. I don't need a fire for that. I just need to be around Nathan for my body to heat up.

He turns around and grins when he sees me standing there, nervous but excited as I try to act natural with my hands, but failing miserably.

"Let me give you the tour."

I nod as my mouth waters. "Okay. Where should we start?"

His eyes get that ravenous look again as he looks me up and down. "The master bedroom."

I gulp. "Sounds like a perfect place to start."

He walks over and takes my hand in his, swallowing it in his big palm.

"There's an inground pool under all that snow," he says.

"Too bad," I kid. "I didn't bring my bathing suit."

He smiles as his eyebrow raises. "Like I would let you wear one anyway."

My cheeks heat up as we head to the stairs. Soft lights pop on whenever we walk down the hallway or into a room. This house is as high-tech as it comes.

"You have so many rooms in this house," I say as we pass yet another guest room.

"I want to have *lots* of kids," he tells me. "I'm going to be stuffing your little belly full of them. Are you ready for that?"

I swallow as I slide my hands over my stomach, imaging what it would feel like to have Nathan's seed growing in my womb. To have a child together. To start a real family.

I glance over my shoulder down the hallway and smile when I picture little feet running after us, excited for Christmas morning, tucking them in with dreams of sugarplums dancing in their heads.

"I'm ready for that," I admit. It just comes out, but once the words are spoken, I know that they're true.

I want those experiences with Nathan. I want to give him the family he's been waiting for. The family we've both been waiting for.

I'll do that for him. I'll do it for me. For us.

He steps in close and that protective arm slides around

my side, his big palm on my back, holding me against him. "I love you," he whispers.

It's crazy, but isn't love always crazy? Does it ever make sense?

Love is heart territory. It doesn't have to make sense to the brain.

"I love you too," I tell him.

He kisses me hard and lovingly with all the swirling emotions that we're both feeling expressed in a long sensual beautiful kiss.

One that I'll never forget.

I gasp as he suddenly leans down and picks me up.

He throws me over his shoulder and I'm suddenly weightless as he carries me into his room.

I can feel my eyes widening as he throws me onto his huge bed. There's a fireplace in this room too, but this one just takes a switch to turn on. The fire explodes to life as Nathan hits it with his elbow.

I watch with my heart racing in anticipation as he slowly slips out one button at a time on his shirt. His massive chiseled chest is full of sexy ink. I find myself moving up, trying to get a better view as each button comes undone.

Finally, he gets to the bottom and the white fitted shirt splits down the middle. His shredded abs flex and clench as he pulls the shirt back and peels it off his muscular arms.

God, he's hot.

Hot doesn't even explain it. Hot is the roaring fire behind him. This man is scorching. I feel myself melting in his presence as I watch him in wonder.

"You're my family now," he says as those big hands get

to work on his belt. "You'll never be alone again, Holly. I promise it."

It's just the words I need to hear. I get all choked up as I nod to him, knowing he's telling the truth.

He lets his pants drop and steps out of them. Is it just me or does that cock seem to be getting bigger every time I encounter it?

It looks monstrous all caged up in his boxer briefs—hard and raging to come out and devour an innocent little virgin like me.

I inhale deeply as Nathan comes forward, the intensity in his eyes making me weak, making me powerless, making me feel invincible.

There's nothing I can do but submit to him.

Just like we've both been waiting for.

CHAPTER EIGHT

Nate

"Finally," I whisper to myself as I lower the zipper on Holly's dress.

She's on her knees on the bed with her back to me, that long brown hair tucked over her shoulder.

I slowly drag the zipper down, my heart beating harder with every inch it travels. Her skin looks so smooth, I just want to lick every inch of her. A groan tumbles out of my throat when the zipper passes her lacy black bra.

I've been dying all night to see my girl's chest with nothing covering it and I'm only a few painful seconds away from seeing it with my own eyes.

The zipper goes as far as it can, the adorable little crack of her ass barely visible under the dress. My cock throbs harder as I unwrap the priceless Christmas present the universe has given me. I'm already treasuring her.

"Stand up," I command as I slide my palm down her arm and grab her hand. Her fingers tighten around mine and she gets up to her feet, standing on the bed.

Her back is to me as her dress tumbles down to her ankles. She smells so good. Looks even better.

My eyes travel down the curve of her back to her sexy panties that are right in front of my face. I lick my lips as my hungry eyes roam over her beautiful ass.

I can't help but touch it, running my hand over her right cheek before slipping down and sliding my hand over her mound. She's so wet. I can feel her warm juices seeping through the thin lacy material.

She whimpers as I touch her pussy and then whimpers louder as I take my hand away.

"What's the matter?" I ask in a deep throaty voice. "You want my hand back on your pussy?"

"*Yes*," she moans.

"You didn't say please…"

"*Please*," she begs.

"That will come," I promise as I slide my hands along her smooth hips and dip my fingers underneath the straps of her panties. "We got to get you naked first."

She tilts her ass back to me as I slowly pull her panties down. My eyes are locked on the crack of her ass as I tug them down. My mouth waters as I watch her pretty little asshole come into view and then the wet pink lips of her juicy cunt.

"That's a good girl," I say as I slide them down her legs. "Do you like when I play with your pussy?"

Her hands are in her hair as the lust builds and starts to make her crazy. "I fucking *love* it."

"Not so innocent anymore, are we?" I say with a grin

as I guide her beautiful feet out of her wet panties. "What have I done to you?"

"I don't know," she whines with desperation in her raspy voice. "I can't stop thinking about your giant cock."

That's just what I like to hear.

I grin, knowing I got her now.

My Christmas Holly is as addicted to me as I am to her. Just where I want her.

"And where do you want my giant cock?" I slowly slide my hand up the inside of her leg, stopping on her upper inner thigh, just before her cunt. I guess I'm a cruel fucker who likes to tease my girl.

She whines as her hips gyrate, trying to get her burning cunt onto my hand. Not going to happen. Not yet.

"I want it…"

"Tell me."

She sucks in a breath as she jerks her head back, her long hair tumbling down her back. "I want it… deep inside me."

"Where?"

"In my pussy. *Deep* in my pussy."

My cock is throbbing as I guide her down to her knees. It's taking everything I have not to forcefully bend her over and fuck her hard right now. But I want to take it slow. Draw it out. Torture her a little bit before I give her all the pleasure in the world.

"You'll get my cock when it's time for your virgin pussy to get my cock."

She moans in anticipation as I unclasp her bra and slide it off her shoulders.

"I've been waiting to see these beautiful tits all night," I say as her bra slips off and she covers her breasts with her arm. "Turn around and show your man what he's been waiting for."

She turns around on the bed, still on her knees as she watches me with glassy 'fuck me' eyes. Her arm is covering her nipples, but the flesh pouring over her forearm is enough to make me ravenous.

"Drop your arm," I command. "Show me your tits."

She nibbles on her bottom lip as she lowers her arm. My body tightens, ready to pounce, ready to claim this virgin's cherry and devour her whole. I struggle to hold back and take a second to admire her beautiful perky breasts.

I'm the first man to see them and I want to take my time enjoying the sight.

They're stunning just like the rest of her. Small, but perky with firm pink nipples sticking up invitingly. I lick my lips as I go to her, grabbing her hips as I put my mouth on them. Her fingers slide into my hair as I suck on one then the other, taking my time as I explore her curves and make her moan.

My girl grows impatient and grabs my wrist with a firm grip. I smile as she yanks my hand between her legs and puts it on her cunt. She's so *wet*. Her hot cream is coating my fingers as I play with her kitty.

The need to breed this girl comes back with a vengeance. It's stronger than ever.

All the control I've been desperately clinging onto snaps.

It's time.

I'm taking this girl's innocence. Her cherry. Her womb. I'm taking it all with my raw cock.

She gasps in surprise as I grab the back of her thighs

and pull up. She falls backward and lands on the bed with a giggle.

That giggle quickly fades when she realizes what's happening—she's on her back, naked, legs spread, with a big hard cock ready to vigorously fuck her like an animal.

"You still want this monster deep inside you?" I ask as I wrap my hand around my thick shaft and bring it to her pussy lips.

She can't talk right now. Her glassy eyes are fixated on my dick, words unable to form. She nods instead.

That's good enough for me.

She writhes on the bed like a filthy little whore as I drag the swollen head of my cock through her wet lips, parting them to reveal the virgin pink inside.

"Such a good girl," I whisper as I test out her hole, pressing my head against it.

I shudder all over when I feel how tight she is. "This hot little pussy keeps getting tighter as the night goes on."

She's writhing on the bed, pulling up the sheets, hair flayed out around her, eyes squeezed closed, back arching and flattening as she whines and whimpers. "*Please*," she begs. "*Please*, Nathan. Stick it in me. I'm fucking dying without you…"

I take one last look at her beautiful virgin pussy, knowing it's never going to be this pure again. I'm going to fuck the purity out of it.

"Okay," I tell her. "I'll give you what you want."

I lean down and give her pussy a soft kiss before standing back up, feet planted on the floor, and grab her trembling legs. She gasps as I yank her toward me.

My hard cock falls onto her spread cunt and she moans as she plays with her tits.

"Pinch those nipples for me," I command and she does, squeezing them in her fingers as I grab my dick.

We both freeze, hearts stopped in our chests, as I press my head against her tight wet opening and push in.

Fuck… She's so goddamn tight. Her cunt squeezes and clenches the head of my cock as I force it in.

My eyes are locked where we're connected as I slide in another inch, her warm cream oozing out and dripping along my thick shaft.

"You're doing so good, baby. How does it feel?"

"*Big*," she moans. "Big, but good."

"Just try and relax," I say as I begin to rub her clit with my thumb, helping to loosen her up. "We still have a long way to go. You're doing so well. I'm going to put it *deep* inside you."

Her hips start to grind against me as I play with her engorged clit. She likes that. A lot.

My body tenses when I come up to her cherry, fresh and still intact inside her virgin cunt. It's mine. I'm taking it.

I growl as I thrust through it and plunge my cock all the way inside her sexy body. She cries out, but she also wraps her legs around me, holding me in, keeping me deep inside her where I belong.

"Your pussy feels so fucking good," I groan as I feel her soft warmth clenching and milking me. This cunt is brutally tight, choking my cock like it's trying to end its life. I fucking love it.

She whimpers as I begin to pull back out slowly. I'm loving the way my cock is covered in her cream. I never want to wipe it off. I always want to be covered in her.

"There's my angel," I say as I start to slide back in.

"This is what you wanted. What you begged for. I need you to tell me how much you love my big dick."

"*Oh fuck,*" she moans, back arching with each inch I give her.

"Tell me."

"I love your big dick."

Her filthy words sends a burst of heat searing through me.

"Say it again."

"I love your cock," she moans as she squeezes her tits and writhes in front of me. "I can't get enough of it stretching me out. It's so fucking big. It's so fucking good."

"That's my girl," I say as I start to thrust in and out harder. Her pussy is nice and slick, taking me easier as I pound into her at a firm, steady pace.

"I know you love it," I groan as I watch my cock splitting through her wet lips. "Look how wet you are. Making a mess all over your man's dick."

I yank it out and she nearly cries. "Come here," I command as I hold it up for her to see. "Come lick this mess clean. Come taste how fresh your pussy is."

She bounds up to her knees and grabs my wet dick out of my hand. Without a second of hesitation, she shoves it deep into her mouth and moans as she licks me clean.

My heart is pounding in my chest. Pleasure aching through my body as I feel her hot tongue wrap around me and drag up my shaft. She cups my balls in her hand and I nearly cum in her mouth.

"That's good," I tell her as I pull my clean cock out of her mouth. "You're going to make me cum if your sexy mouth keeps that up."

"Cum down my throat," she begs as she tries to get my dick in her mouth again. "I want to taste you."

I gently push her slutty little hand away. "Later. This big load is destined for your pussy, angel. I want to coat your ripe womb with it."

Her blue eyes sparkle as she looks at me in surprise.

"That's right, baby. I'm fucking you raw and claiming your body in *every* way. I want my child growing inside you. What do you think about that?"

There are no words. She just drops back onto the bed and spreads her legs for me. Her hand slides down her belly and she begins playing with her clit as she watches me with a sexy, challenging look.

"I think you want it," I say as I go back to her.

My cock slides in easier this time. Her pussy is no longer trying to force me back out with its tightness. It's welcoming me and taking me in.

The restraint I've been dealing with all night snaps and I'm all animal now. I fuck her *hard*. Ruthlessly. Mercilessly. Hard pounding thrusts into her tight heat that has the bed jerking around and has her tits swaying back and forth.

She's crying out and grabbing the sheets as I let her pussy have it. *Harder*. *Faster*. I'm fucking her like a madman as I slam my cock into her over and over again.

"*Yes!*" she screams. "Yes, Nathan! Fuck me! Cum in me!"

"We're going to cum together," I tell her in a firm dominant voice. "When I count down to one."

"*Fuck*," she moans as her eyes run over my flexed tattooed chest. "I can't wait that long! I'm going to cum now!"

"You want me to keep fucking you?"

"*Yes!*" She's desperate now. I can tell she's so close, barely hanging on.

"Then you're going to wait until I count down to one," I tell her in a forceful voice. "You can do it, baby. Let's go.

"Ten."

"*Oh shit*. I can't…"

"You will. I've been waiting for this moment all of my life, you can wait ten measly seconds."

She sucks in a breath, her face twisted up in agony as I thrust my cock in and out of her cunt.

"Nine."

"Oh, Nathan… It feels so good."

"Eight."

Her teeth are gritted, my arms flexed.

"Your pussy feels so good, angel. I'm so fucking close. Seven."

She grabs her tits and pulls them as her body twists on the bed. Her legs are shaking around me.

"Six."

"Oh, fuck. *Fuck!*"

"Hang in there, baby. It's almost over. Five."

I'm thrusting into her hard and fast, picking up speed and intensity the lower I count.

"Four."

"*Shit.*"

"I want to cum too," I groan, feeling desperate for any kind of release.

"Three."

She moans hard.

"Almost there, baby. Get ready."

Her mouth opens, but nothing comes out.

"Watch me fucking you as we cum," I command her. "I want to see those sexy blue eyes on me."

She opens them with a shudder and watches with her

eyelids half-closed as I slam my cock into her at a vigorous pace.

"Two."

The pressure building in me is about to snap. I can barely hold it back. I'm going to cum so hard.

"One. Cum with me."

We both let go and it's fucking heaven. I ram my cock into her and hold it in as we both cry out in bliss.

Her pussy tightens and clenches my pulsing shaft, the first time this virgin cunt has ever came on a cock. It's a beautiful sight, watching my angel thrash around on the bed, feeling more euphoria running through her veins than she'd ever thought possible.

I love being the cause of her pleasure and I love that she's the cause of mine.

My cum surges out, coating her insides and drenching her ripe womb with my seed.

"That's my girl," I whisper to her as she wraps her shaking legs around me. She opens her arms and I go to her, embracing her as I begin to gently slide in and out slowly, a few more strokes before I have to pull out of her still pulsing heat.

The clock catches my eye and I realize that it's well after midnight.

"Merry Christmas, Holly," I whisper on her lips.

She tilts her head up and kisses me. "Merry Christmas, Nathan."

"The first together, but not the last."

Her blue eyes are shining as she watches me, knowing I'm right, knowing we'll be together for every Christmas doing exactly this from here on out.

Hopefully with a lot of babies sleeping down the hall.

CHAPTER NINE

Holly

It's still snowing in the morning. There's no better feeling than waking up to fat snowflakes falling outside on Christmas day. Well, maybe one better feeling…

And that's waking up with Nathan's big protective arms wrapped around me and feeling his long hard cock pressed against my thigh. I inhale deeply, smelling him with a moan. I could get used to this. This bed, this room, this house, this incredible sensation of complete satisfaction, this man, this feeling of being so loved. Of being so lucky. I can get used to it all.

He groans as he stirs and turns around on the bed, taking most of the sheets with him.

His back is to me—huge and carved with muscle. I look so small next to him. I'm half-worried he's going to roll over in the middle of the night and crush me.

With a smile on my face, I crawl up against him and

run my fingertip down his arm, tracing the sexy tattoos. I giggle when I see the goosebumps rising on his skin.

He stirs once more and then opens his eyes.

"Oh, thank God," he says when he sees me. "I thought that was a dream for a second."

"It's reality," I say as I kiss his bare shoulder. "Merry Christmas, Nathan."

He turns and gives me a closed-mouthed kiss on the lips. "Merry Christmas, my Holly."

"Are you ready for your Christmas present?" I ask with a grin on my lips. He smiles as he looks up at me, his eyes half-closed and still sleepy.

"You got me something?"

My hand travels over his round shoulder, down his hard chest, over his rippling abs, and onto his boxer briefs.

"Oh," he groans as he looks down with his interest peaking. My hand is swirling temptingly close to his rock-hard erection.

"Just what I wanted for Christmas," he says in a deep throaty voice. I slide my hand up his long, hard shaft and we both moan at the same time.

His grey boxer briefs are getting a wet spot at the end of his long rod, and it's growing the more I touch him.

Nathan watches as I peel them down, revealing his beautiful candy cane that I just want to spend all day sucking on.

"I've only been awake for five minutes," he says as he watches me wrap my fingers around it. "But I can already tell this is the best Christmas I'm ever going to have."

I'm happier than I've ever been as I watch the look of love on his face while I begin to jerk him off. He sucks in a breath as I stroke his length, up and down with a firm grip.

I lick my palm to get it nice and slick. He groans as he watches my tongue.

His chest flexes as he turns and lets his back drop onto the bed where he can get a better view of the sensual show I'm giving him.

My pussy is already so wet as I stroke him up and down, hard just how he likes it with a steady rhythm.

It's not long before his body begins to buck. I gasp and watch in awe as long streams of hot cum shoot out of his cock all over my hand.

He watches me with hungry lustful eyes as I bring my hand to my mouth and lick his hot mess off my fingers.

"You're beautiful," he says as he slides his hand along my side, over my breast before coming to a stop on my hip. "Absolutely stunning."

I don't have a stitch of clothing on and he's looking at me like a kid who got everything he wanted for Christmas.

I'm about to straddle that big frame and give him even more when I hear the front door open.

"Hello!" someone shouts. "Merry Christmas!"

I grab the sheets with a gasp and hold them against my body. "Who's that?"

Nathan groans as he looks at the clock. "Shit, it's already nine?"

"Who is that?" I repeat.

I jump out of bed and rush over to the window, taking the sheets with me. "There are a ton of cars pulling into your driveway!"

"You said you liked that big family vibe," he says as he starts to get up with a groan. "And it's Christmas…"

I turn to him, feeling my lips curling up into a smile. "Yeah?"

"I guess I forgot to tell you that they're all coming for breakfast."

My pulse starts to race in delight as I bounce up on my bare feet. "Really?!"

"Really. And don't worry, I asked Crystal to bring you some clothes."

A few minutes later, I'm wearing a pair of Crystal's black pants and an ugly Christmas sweater she lent me. It's of my favorite show—Schitt's Creek—and has a picture of David and Moira on it with the words *You Just Fold It In* stitched on the top. I love it and am already planning on buying my own once I can get to a computer.

I rush down the stairs and my face lights up when I see my new family there, all doing family things in the kitchen and living room—arguing about which dish should go into the oven, wives complaining that it's too early for their husbands to start cracking open beers, although they have no objections about taking the mimosas that Nathan is handing out, and kids ogling and touching all of the presents under the tree, trying to find the ones marked for them.

It's like I've stepped into a new life. One that I've been wanting for a long time.

Nathan's cousin is playing Christmas carols on the piano and a few others are singing along. They're good too! It's so festive!

The giant tree is lit up beautifully with a mountain of presents underneath it. I just feel so happy, like my heart is overflowing.

And here comes Nathan, dressed in black pants with an ugly Christmas sweater of his own that says *Santa's Favorite Doctor*.

In all of this wonderful chaos—the shouting, the laughing, the talking, the singing—he's here to ground me, to anchor me, to love me.

I'm so thankful.

And so freaking in love.

I just know I'm going to marry him.

"Ready for your gift?" he whispers into my ear.

"How did you get me anything?" I ask with a laugh. "We haven't left each other's sight since we've met."

He grins. "Come. I have a surprise for you."

Everyone is excited as they follow us to the door. They're all clamoring and pushing to the head to say hi and to wish me a Merry Christmas. My cheeks hurt from smiling, trying to answer each one of them.

"It's outside?" I ask as Nathan opens the front door. Cold air hits me, but it's much warmer than last night. The sun is out and the snowstorm has passed, although it's left all its snow for us to deal with.

A honk echoes down the street and I gasp when I see a brand new Porsche SUV driving down the road. It's as white as the snow with a huge red bow on the hood, blowing in the wind.

I look up at Nathan in shock.

"It's for you," he whispers with a smile.

"How did you—?"

"I told you my sister owns a dealership," he says with a grin. "I called in a favor."

"And you're paying full price, right?" Sandy says. Everyone laughs.

"Yeah, yeah," Nathan says as Sandy's husband turns my new car into the driveway and gets out. "My girl is worth the price."

I don't even know how to act as I walk over to the car

with my head swirling. All these people watching me. Nathan's loving eyes following me.

"I love it," I tell him, not knowing what else to say. "Thank you so much, Nathan. For everything."

"It's just the beginning," he says with a warm smile. "I'm taking care of you now and you'll get everything you need."

I look into his beautiful eyes and for the first time, in a long time, I think that everything is going to work out just fine.

EPILOGUE

Holly

One year later…

"Matthew!" I say as I open the front door with a big smile. "Lian! Merry Christmas!"

Tom rushes over and grabs the presents out of their arms as I step in and give them each a big hug.

It was such a nice surprise four months ago when Matthew returned from Singapore with a brand new wife. I hadn't seen my brother in years but it was a welcome surprise. I was so thrilled to see him.

And the biggest surprise was that I'm going to be an aunt! Lina was five months pregnant and they were both here to stay.

Nathan and his huge clan have become my family over the past year, but there's something special about being close to your blood relatives as well. I always wanted my brother back in my life and I'm so happy and relieved that he's here to stay for good.

"Look at you," Lian says as her eyes drop down to my belly. "Your baby boy is growing so fast."

"I guess he was trying to come out for Christmas," I say with a smile. "He didn't want to miss out on all of the fun. But he's going to have to wait until next year to experience his first Christmas.

"And what about *your* little boy?" I say as we touch each other's bellies. "He's definitely in a growth spurt."

Our due dates are only two weeks apart. I can't tell you how happy I am that my child is going to have cousins nearby to grow up with. Matthew and Lian bought a house down the street with help from Nathan. Our kids are going to be so close as they grow up. They're going to be playing on the block every day.

I was hurt when Matthew came home after abandoning me for all those years, but we talked and worked it out. He apologized and we're closer than ever. And Lian is just great. She's an amazing wife, sister-in-law, and will be a fabulous aunt and mother. I have no doubt.

Nathan and I hang out with them a lot. We must see them at least a few times a week for dinners and game nights.

I'm so thrilled to have them in my life.

"Come on in," I say, waving them into the house. "Grab a drink. There's coffee in the kitchen. Wine, beer, even whiskey if you want to get crazy."

It's only ten in the morning, but hey, it's Christmas. It's happy hour all day!

They step into the house and I close the door to keep the cold out. We're having a huge brunch with all of our friends and family. Our enormous house is already packed full of people and filled with love.

"Need another mimosa?" I ask my father-in-law Mack as I head to the kitchen to check on my man.

"You read my mind," he says with a big grin, shaking his empty glass.

His wife (and my mother-in-law) Linda, slaps his arm. "Get it yourself! She's six months pregnant for God's sake!"

"That's okay," I say with a smile as I grab his glass and waddle into the kitchen. "I don't mind at all!"

I'm just so happy to have everyone here.

Those Christmases on my own were so lonely and depressing. I never want to go back to that. I'm thrilled that my child is going to grow up in a big family full of love. I hope he never knows the loneliness that I experienced. The loneliness that Nathan took away forever.

I step into the kitchen and my eyes dart right to my man. I'm always aware of where he is in a crowd. I still can't seem to get my eyes to wander away from him.

He's standing in front of the stove flipping pancakes with a black apron strapped around his big muscular body.

I grin as I walk up to him and slip a hand into the front pocket.

"Ooooh, what's cooking in here?" I ask him with a flirty, raspy voice. "Anything in here for me?"

"I always got something cooking for you," he says as he looks over his shoulder at me with a salacious grin on his devilish face.

I love that look. It always gets me going. And with the pregnancy hormones, it's been easier than ever. We can't seem to keep our insatiable hands off one another.

It's been a year and a few hours since we first came crashing into each other's lives. A lot has happened during that time.

We fell in love. We got married. We got pregnant. And we got started on our long journey together that will hopefully never end. I guess it will one day when we're old and grey and way too wrinkly, but for now, we have our youth, we have our love, and we have each other.

It's all we need.

Nathan drops the spatula onto the counter and turns around. I smile as he swallows me in his big comforting arms. "Want me to kick everyone out?" he whispers.

"What a tempting thought…"

We could kick everyone out… strip down in front of the Christmas tree, fool around on the way up the stairs, slip into bed, and spend the rest of the day with my man's monstrous cock lodged deep inside of me.

Mmmmmm… I'm almost sold on the idea…

But we have guests and it is Christmas.

We're just going to have to wait. Isn't that the best part of Christmas anyway? The waiting… To open presents, for Santa to come, for my man to cum?

I give him a little peck on the lips and then put the spatula back in his hand. "Later, you can unwrap me all you want."

He groans as I turn him around back to his burning pancakes. "You're killing me, angel."

I slap his hard ass and head over to the mimosa station with a giggle.

I'm still thinking of all the tempting possibilities as I fill my father-in-law's glass with orange juice and champagne. This is a large house… lot's of rooms to get lost in…

Stop it. It's Christmas and you're surrounded by family.

I shake my head and laugh as I head back into the living room. To think that last year, I was an innocent virgin who hadn't even experienced her first kiss. Nathan has corrupted me in every way. I'm no longer innocent and I'm definitely no longer a virgin. I'm a dirty insatiable slut when it comes to him.

I try to tamp down the filthy thoughts in my head as I walk back into the room, smiling at all of my guests.

"Love that sweater," I say to Josh as I look at his ugly Christmas sweater. It's a picture of Santa spanking a stripper over his knee and it says '*I do it for the ho's.*'

Everyone looks like they're having a great time—laughing, smiling, and joking around. The Christmas tree is the biggest I've ever seen in a house and it's lit up spectacularly with a gorgeous porcelain angel on top. Nathan came home with it last week, saying it reminded him of me. There are a ton of presents laid at the bottom and I wouldn't be surprised if most of them were for me. My man *loves* to spoil me rotten.

My heart feels like it's going to burst as I look around. It's a proper Christmas. A true Christmas. A Christmas full of love.

I'm so happy I get to share it with all of these wonderful people.

And I'm so happy it's only gonna last a couple of hours…

I'm excited to do whatever is on Nathan's dirty mind. I bet it's something good. Something worth waiting for.

Once everyone leaves, it will be time to have some *real* Christmas fun.

I can't wait!

EPILOGUE

Nate

Thirty years later…

"Ho, ho, ho," I holler as I step into the room, ringing the bells in my white-gloved hand.

All six of my grandkids perk up, eyes as wide as saucers. They're sitting in front of the Christmas tree, but bounce up and rush toward me as I put down my huge red bag full of presents. I'm dressed as Santa Claus, big white beard and everything. I would have grown it out for real, but Holly loves my cheeks nice and smooth, so what was I going to do? Disappoint my wife? Never.

"Hi, Santa," Holly says in a flirty voice as she comes over and plants a kiss on my cheek. "I thought you'd never get here."

She giggles as I lean into her ear. "You know I'm

always up for sliding into your chimney," I whisper only loud enough for her to hear.

After all these decades, I can still get her adorable cheeks to turn red.

Our five kids and their spouses groan as I kiss her neck.

"Keep it clean, Santa!" my oldest daughter Camilla says with a shake of her head. "It's Christmas."

"You know Santa loves his sugar," I say in a booming Santa voice. "And I always want a piece of Holly on Christmas day."

"You'll get a piece tonight," Holly whispers to me.

"I want the whole thing," I practically growl back.

"The kids, *Santa*," our youngest Martin says as he shakes his head. "Hand out the presents."

"Presents!" I bellow as I pick up my bag. The kids at my feet stir with excitement. They're looking up at me with big smiles on their cute little faces. They remind me of my children—their parents—when they were young and full of wonder.

A lifetime of amazing memories come rushing back to me. I've had quite the life with Holly by my side.

Springs, and summers, and autumns, but the Holiday season is our favorite time of year. It reminds us of the day we met and it all changed.

When she became part of my life and part of my family.

When she became everything to me.

The kids squeal in excitement as I hand out the presents. It's not long before the bag is empty and they're all gone, unwrapping their gifts by the tree.

"Come sit on my lap," I tell my wife as I sit down in

the rocking chair. "And tell Santa what you want for Christmas."

Our kids groan and cover their eyes as Holly bounds over with a spring in her step and sits on my lap. They should be lucky to have what we have when they're our age.

Holly wraps her arm around my shoulder and leans in, those soft breasts pushing into my chest.

"That's not a candy cane in my pocket," I whisper to her.

She giggles. "You read my mind. That's what I was going to ask for. That's what I've been craving."

"Should we kick everyone out?" I ask with a grin.

She gives me a sweet smile and I nearly die. She's never been more beautiful to me. She turned fifty-three this year and she's still a stunner. Still a knockout. Still gets me going with one look.

"It's Christmas," she says as she gives me a playful slap on the arm. "We're not kicking everyone out. But we can meet up in the laundry room… ten minutes?"

I grin as she stands up and smooths out her dress. "Make it five."

She gives me a wink as she bounds off into the kitchen.

"Are you going to stay for dinner, Santa?" one of my grandkids Amanda asks.

I shake my head with a grin. "No, I can't. Santa has a date."

"With who?"

"With the best woman in the world," I tell her. "Mrs. Clause."

They all wave with a cheery goodbye as I leave, bellowing ho ho ho.

I'm grinning as I exit, excited to meet up with my sexy ho ho ho in the laundry room.

The magic is about to begin because I'm getting a Holly for Christmas.

The End!

MORE CHRISTMAS BOOKS BY OTT

Available at www.OliviaTTurner.com

COME AND JOIN MY PRIVATE
FACEBOOK GROUP!

Become an OTT Lover!

www.facebook.com/groups/OTTLovers

BECOME OBSESSED WITH OTT

Sign up to my mailing list for all the latest OTT news and get a free book that you can't find anywhere else!

OBSESSED
By Olivia T. Turner
A Mailing List Exclusive!

When I look out my office window and see her in the next building, I know I have to have her.

I buy the whole damn company she works for just to be near her.

She's going to be in my office working under me.

Under, over, sideways—we're going to be working together in *every* position.

This young innocent girl is going to find out that I work my employees *hard*.

And that her new rich CEO is already beyond *obsessed* with her.

This dominant and powerful CEO will have you begging for overtime! Is it just me or is there nothing better than a hot muscular alpha in a suit and tie!

All my books are SAFE with zero cheating and a guaranteed sweet HEA. Enjoy!

Go to www.OliviaTTurner.com to get your free ebook of Obsessed

AUDIOBOOKS

Check out my complete collection of audiobooks at
www.OliviaTTurner.com!

I'm adding more of your favorite OTT stories all the time!

DON'T BE SHY. COME FOLLOW ME...
I WON'T BITE UNLESS YOU ASK ME TO

www.OliviaTTurner.com

- facebook.com/OliviaTTurnerAuthor
- instagram.com/authoroliviatturner
- goodreads.com/OliviaTTurner
- amazon.com/author/oliviatturner
- bookbub.com/authors/olivia-t-turner

SNOW PLACE LIKE HOME
TWO CHAPTER SAMPLE

CHAPTER ONE

Mandy

"What are these supposed to be?" I ask with a laugh as Christine puts the tray of cookies on the counter.

"Candy canes," Christine answers with her shoulders slumped down.

They've melted into phallic shapes. I pick up one that looks especially bad and laugh. "It looks like a Christmas treat, but it's no candy cane."

She snatches it out of my hand and places it back on the tray. "It's Christmas, get your mind out of the gutter. They'll look fine after we put icing all over it."

"Yes, let's cover it with white icing because *that* will make it look less like a cock."

Christine laughs as she mixes the bowl of red icing. "I missed you so much! How many more years of college?"

"Two," I say with a sigh. I didn't realize how much I

missed being home until I came home for the Christmas holidays. It feels like forever since I've hung out with my best friend.

"What am I supposed to do until then?" she asks, looking depressed.

I smile sadly at her. "You'll always have your penis cookies."

We both laugh as Mariah Carey belts out some high notes in the background. Christmas at Christine's has always been a huge affair. Every inch of her parent's house is decorated with something Christmas related. They even decorate *inside* the garage. They devote a full room in the basement to storing all of their Christmas stuff and it comes out on October 1st. Every year for Halloween, Christine's house is decorated as the North Pole and her parents are Mr. & Mrs. Clause. The kids in the neighborhood love it.

"So," Christine whispers. "Tell me about the guy sitch."

"Sitch?"

"Situation. I've been cutting off the second half of some words since you've been gone. It's my new thing."

I shake my head as I look at her in shock. "You've changed so much."

"I know. Sometimes I don't even recognize the face in the mirror." We laugh and then she keeps prodding me for some juicy details. "Come on! What's college like? Are you banging a new hot guy named Chad every night? Do people still say bang?"

I wish I had some juicy details for her.

"There's a really hot guy in my Psych class."

"Yeah?" she says, perking up.

"He asked me to borrow a pen."

"Is that like a code word for hooking up?"

"No," I say with a heavy breath. "He just wanted a pen. But when I gave it to him, our hands touched."

She holds the spatula up, her eyes wide with excitement. "And you fell in love?"

"No. That's the end of my story."

Her body slumps down as she stares at me like I've just told her that Santa isn't real. "That's it?"

"Oh, the pen!"

"Yeah?" she asks, perking back up.

"He never gave it back."

"That's the worst story in the history of stories," she says as she turns back to the icing and starts mixing the purple. "Have you hooked up with anyone? It's your second year of college. Don't tell me you still have your V-Card."

I tap my pocket as my cheeks go red. "Still intact."

"What's the point of paying three hundred thousand dollars a year in college tuition if you're not going to bang every guy in sight?"

"Do you have any idea how much college costs?"

"You should be nailing guys around the clock!"

"There's like so much homework and when I'm not studying, I'm working at the coffee shop!"

"Okay, what about there?" she asks, not letting this go. "Do you have any hot coworkers who want to dip their tea bag into your cup?"

"I don't even know what that means."

"It's a metaphor," she says with a salacious grin. "For sex."

I roll my eyes and laugh. Aw, I missed her.

I do have a crush on someone, but it's not on anyone on campus. Or at work.

It's the same crush I've had for the past thirteen years.

Since I was eight years old. It doesn't seem to want to go away.

Matt walks in at the perfect time to save me. He leans over Christine's shoulder and frowns at the cookies. "Penis cookies? Interesting choice for a Christmas Eve party."

"They're candy canes," Christine says as she pushes him away. "You and Dad are supposed to be setting up the bar."

"We are," he says as he opens the fridge and grabs two cans of beer.

"That better be for the bar."

He grins as he walks back out.

"And don't forget the ice!"

"How's it going with Matt?" I ask when he's left the room. Those two have been dating forever. They've been in love since they were ten years old. He's part of the family now and seems to be best friends with Christine's dad.

"Nothing to report," she says with a shrug. "Same old, same old."

We start decorating the phallic-shaped candy canes, trying our best to take the X out of these X-Mas cookies.

"Who's coming tonight?" I ask, trying to sound casual but my heart is hammering inside my chest.

I keep my eyes down on the cookies, but I can feel her watching me suspiciously.

It's the question I've been waiting to ask her since I walked into the house and she gave me a big hug.

"Just the usual," she says. "My parent's friends, our usual high school gang, except Carrie isn't coming."

"Oh, no!"

"She's at her new boyfriend's house this year. Matt's

parents and his sister are coming. Your parents, my cousins, aunts and uncles from my mom's side. Alan and Beth. It should be fun."

I swallow hard as I wonder how far I can push without being too obvious.

"Anyone else?"

I can feel her eyes burning into me as I slather purple icing onto the world's ugliest candy cane cookie.

"Anyone in particular?" she asks, tilting her head as she watches me.

Oh, shit. I can feel my cheeks getting all hot.

"Someone like… Uncle Ethan?"

I look up at her and gulp. Guilty as charged.

"You're not still into him?"

I open my mouth to deny it, but a weird gurgle comes out instead. I've been in love with Christine's uncle for my entire life. It was actually since I was eight years old, but it feels like forever.

He's her dad's younger brother and he's the hottest man I've ever seen.

I can still remember the first time I saw him like it was yesterday. It was summer and Christine and I were playing in her pool when the loudest rumbling I've ever heard thundered down the street.

I watched in awe as Ethan pulled up on his motorcycle. Christine jumped out of the pool and ran up to him, giving him a wet hug as I watched with my little heart pumping on overdrive. I couldn't believe how beautiful he was. He was tall with a wide frame and big muscular arms. I didn't understand why I couldn't stop staring at them. His hair was long back then, almost to his shoulders, but thankfully, he cut it.

I can still remember marveling at the beautifully intricate tattoos on his round chest and big shoulders as he jumped into the pool to play with us. He threw us is into the air over and over again and I remember screaming, thinking I was flying higher than the house before I landed in the water and swam back to him for more.

One thing was for sure… I was in love.

And that crush on Ethan Hearst was cemented into my heart.

"Mandy!" Christine shouts. "You're pouring sprinkles all over the counter!"

"Shit! Sorry!"

"You were thinking about my uncle weren't you?"

"What?! No!"

"You had a distant look in your eye and a creepy little pervy smile on your face. You were thinking about Uncle Ethan!"

"I was not! I was thinking about… homework."

"Homework? You're on break for the Holidays. Your semester is over. You don't have homework."

"That's what I was thinking about. I was happy I don't have any."

She frowns as she looks at me skeptically.

"Don't fuck my uncle. Please. It's Christmas."

"So… does that mean he's coming?"

Her forehead gets all wrinkly as she frowns even harder. "Yes, he's coming. But he's off-limits."

I feel like my heart is going to explode out of my chest.

"Chris, I would never," I say, acting all indignant.

She puts her hand up, shutting me up real fast. "Okay, slut. Save the goodie two shoes act. I know you too well for that."

She shakes her head as she gets back to the cookies.

Meanwhile, I'm going through different outfits in my head, trying to pick out the perfect one for tonight. Something that will get me put on the naughty list.

And I have just the thing…

CHAPTER TWO

Mandy

"Whoa, Mandy! That's *a lot* of cleavage!" The first words my mother says to me when I see her at the party.

I look down and self-consciously fix my red dress. "It's not that bad."

It's not!

I'm not in slutty territory yet, but I might look like I want to get my bells jingled this Holiday season.

My father just frowns and quickly wanders off.

"You're just used to me in sweat pants and ponytails," I tell my mother.

"Maybe," she says as she looks me up and down. I'm wearing a tight red dress that's a tad on the low cut end, but it makes my rack look magnificent. At least, that's what Christine said when she helped me pick it out. "You do look beautiful. So grown up."

That's what I'm hoping Ethan is going to think when

he sees me. I want him to see me as a grown up woman and not as Christine's cute little friend whose name I can't quite remember.

My eyes keep darting to the door every time it opens. *Damn.* It's just Christine's aunt and uncle from her mom's side.

I wander into the kitchen and ask Christine's mom if she needs help with anything. She's one of those amazing hostesses who can do a dozen things at the same time while having a fully engaged conversation and make it look effortless and fun.

"Pass this tray of appetizers around, will you, dear?" she asks as she hands me the spinach dip with a bowl of nachos. "I *love* that dress. How are you still single?"

"Mandy is very *mature* when it comes to her taste in guys," Christine says with a smirk as she picks a nacho from my bowl.

"I'm sure there's lots of mature boys in college to pick from," Mrs. Hearst says as she takes a tray of spanakopitas out of the oven.

"Don't harass her and twist her arm, Mom," Christine says as she reaches for the spinach dip, "or she might say uncle."

I yank the bowl away from her before she can dip her chip. She laughs as I stick my tongue out and hurry out of the kitchen.

I make my way around the crowded room, chatting lightly with everyone as I offer them chips and dip.

"Mandy," Christine's older cousin Randy says with a pervy grin as he looks me up and down. "Haven't seen you in a while. You're all grown up."

"So, are you," I say as I glance down at his huge bulging stomach. He was always the most annoying of her cousins. When he wasn't wiping his nose on the couch or kicking someone, he was usually ruining whatever game we were playing by cheating and taking temper tantrums.

He grabs an empty wine glass from the counter and fills it halfway with a bottle of red (that I'm sure he didn't bring).

"I hear you're going to college," he says. "Isn't that cute?"

"And I hear you're still unemployed. That's cute too." He got fired from his last job at a gas station because he took a temper tantrum and flipped over the gum display. Classic Randy.

The door opens again and I whip my head around, hoping it's Ethan.

This time, I'm not disappointed. At all.

My lifelong crush walks in wearing a long gray coat with a dark red scarf wrapped tightly around his neck. There's an expensive-looking bottle of wine in his hands, and an image of the two of us sitting in front of a roaring fireplace as he opens a similar bottle flashes into my head.

I clear my throat and shake the fantasy out of my mind. I don't want to miss any of this. He's dusted with light snow from his big arms, to his shoulders, to his medium-length hair that's looking grayer than the last time I saw him.

"Hold this," I say as I shove the two bowls into Randy's chest. He balances them awkwardly in his arms as he stares at me in shock. I grab the glass of wine from his hand and chug the entire thing as I stare at Ethan over the rim.

It warms my body and soothes the nervous jitters I'm feeling as my Christmas dream comes true.

"What am I supposed to do with this?" Randy asks.

"Eat it. I don't care," I answer as I walk along the wall with my eyes on Ethan like I'm stalking him.

Christine's dad greets him at the door and takes his coat. My eyes are locked on him as he peels off his scarf, revealing his thick neck with the sexy black and gray tattoo running up the side. I already know that it goes all the way over his right shoulder and halfway down his arm. I've fantasized about that tattoo for way too many hours. I've had conversations with it in my mind.

I take a breath of relief when Mr. Hearst closes the door behind him. He didn't bring a girl. He's single too.

"Hey, Mandy," Jeannie, a friend from high school says. "Did you hear that I'm pregnant?"

"That's great," I mumble as I keep moving. I don't want anything to ruin this moment. I have a clear view of Ethan getting partially undressed and I'm not going to spoil it because Jeannie got herself knocked up.

He was always a great dresser. Always in style, or even a little ahead of the current trends.

Tonight, he's wearing dark jeans and a sexy tweed blazer that molds to his beautiful muscular frame. Under that, he's wearing a white collared shirt with a tight navy blue sweater over it. Under all that is hard carved muscles covered in sexy ink.

"Mandy!" Christine's neighbor says, making me jump so high I nearly get airborne. He laughs. "A little jumpy there, are we?"

"Hi, Mr. Rhodes. It's nice to see you again."

I try to be polite, but my eyes keep darting over to Ethan as he works his way through the crowd, saying hi to everyone and flashing that knee-weakening smile.

"I haven't seen you around lately."

"College," I say with a smile. "I'm just back for the Holidays."

I always liked Mr. & Mrs. Rhodes. They gave out full-length chocolate bars on Halloween and never minded us climbing their fence whenever we kicked a ball or hit a badminton birdie over it.

My eye follows Ethan through the room as we chat for a bit about my classes and then about his new pool.

When Ethan disappears into the kitchen, I get all jittery and excuse myself.

I swing back to Randy who's eating all the chips and spinach dip by himself. "Give me that," I say as I yank the bowls out of his hands. "I didn't mean literally eat them all. They were to pass around."

He looks at me with confusion—spinach dip dripping from his chin—as I storm off into the kitchen.

I stop with a gasp when I see Ethan hugging Christine's mom in the kitchen. She has her hand on his wide back (the lucky bitch) as she tells him to grab a beer from the cooler on the deck.

I'm just standing there, holding the two bowls and gawking at him as he opens the sliding doors, leans over, and fishes a beer out of the cooler.

"Have you no shame?" Christine whispers as she walks over, shaking her head. "Ogling my guest slash uncle's ass?"

"I wasn't ogling," I whisper back, but even as I say it, I can't seem to rip my eyes away from his ass.

She just laughs and heads over to him. "Hey, Uncle Ethan," she says as she gives him a hug.

His face lights up when he sees her. "Hey, Chrissy!" he says as he wraps his big arms around her. He's the only person in the world who can call Christine Chrissy and live to tell about it. "How have you been? Has Matt proposed yet?"

He takes her hand and looks at her empty finger. "Nope. But he is buying me a bird feeder for Christmas, so there's that. I saw it in his closet."

"Birds are nice," Ethan says with a sympathetic shrug.

I leap forward, desperate for an opening. "I like birds!" I say nervously. Christine grins as she watches me flounder pathetically. "Penguins. Ostriches. Sparrows." I gulp. "Seagulls."

Oh, crap. I'm really starting to sweat now. Ethan is staring right at me!

I have to save this disaster of a moment. "What is your favorite bird, Uncle Ethan? I mean, Ethan!"

Christine snorts out a laugh as she looks up at him. "You remember my friend, Mandy?"

He's holding his breath as he looks at me with the sexiest brown eyes I've ever seen. "I do," he says, his voice deeper and raspier than before.

"I have to go get some wine bottles from the garage," Christine says as Ethan's heated eyes lock onto mine. "I'll leave you with Mandy to talk some more about... birds."

She leaves with a laughing snort and it's just the two of us standing here. He has new lines on the sides of his eyes, but they suit him. He's not clean-shaven like the last time I saw him three years ago. He has salt and pepper stubble all over his cheeks and chin. I swallow hard imagining what it would feel like against my smooth cheek, or better yet, rubbing against the inside of my thighs.

He's so frigging *hot*. This man gets hotter as the years go by.

And for this moment, he's all mine.

I screwed up my opening, so it can only get better from here.
Right?
Gulp.

Get the full copy on Amazon!

Printed in Great Britain
by Amazon